TOP
OF THE
WORLDS

Dana Burkey

First of all I would like to say a big thank you to Bows By April for the beautiful TNT Force bow featured on the cover. Also a massive thank you to Dehen cheer for the Nitro uniform, and to CheerBowsBowtique for the Worlds Bid bow, both featured on the back cover.

Next I would like to dedicate this book to all of the amazing cheerleaders, cheer moms, and friends I have made this cheer season. You have all helped inspire me to keep creating and staying extra sparkly. Special shout out to Kylie, Vicky, Lauryn, Sidney, McKenna, Savannah, Katie, Tori, Brooke, Kristina, Landon, Lexi, Madeline, Clara Joyce, Aspen, Jasmine, Garrett, and many more!

Finally, a special shout out to Peyton for being my partner in crime all cheer season as well as my vlogging buddy. Riding escalators with you will always be my favorite part of Spirit Cheer!

CHAPTER 1

"Time to get up Max, or we're going to be late."

With a groan, I rolled over in my bed, reaching to grab my phone off my nightstand. I expected to quickly do the math on how much longer I had until my alarm was going to go off, but was shocked to see it was almost 10 am. Sitting up and hopping out of bed in one swift movement, I scrolled through my phone to see I had missed my alarm, a few text messages, and even a call from my best friend Lexi.

"How did this happen?" I muttered the words to myself as I tossed my phone onto my bed and raced into my closet. I could hear a not so happy cat run out of it thanks to the sudden wake up, but I had other things to worry about. Pulling off my pajamas, I quickly slipped on my black shorts and black tank top that were thankfully sitting on my sparkly teal backpack. Inside the bag were my shoes, uniform, and everything else I needed for the day. Or rather everything but my makeup and hair products. I quickly grabbed those items from my bathroom before all but running into the kitchen where my dad sat drinking coffee.

"I'm ready," I said, before setting my bag down and racing back into my room to grab socks. When I returned a few seconds later my dad was laughing.

"Spark performs in an hour and a half, so we have plenty of time," he explained between his laughter. "Why don't you sit for a minute and eat breakfast. I'll load up the car."

Nodding, I moved to pour myself a bowl of cereal, pausing to head into my room yet again when I remembered my phone sitting on my bed. Once I was finally sitting at the table, I was able to calm down. At least as much as I could. It helped when I saw most of the missed texts were just ones I didn't read from the night before. They were about plans for slumber parties and other fun get-togethers over the next week and were most of the reason why I was up late enough to miss my alarms. I replied to a few of the messages, then updated my Instagram and Snapchats before my dad returned.

"You might want a coat," he said, sitting down to once again drink from his coffee mug. "It's not raining much anymore but it's still pretty chilly."

I nodded, making the mental note to grab another layer on my way to the car. I knew my teal team hoodie was hanging up in my room, which would make my dad and I match. Although people often told me I looked a lot like my dad, I knew I got most of my looks from my mom. Sure, I had my dad's dark brown hair, but my eyes were nothing like the grey-green of his. Instead, my blue eyes matched my mom's, although mine were a brighter blue than all the memories and photos I have of her from before she died. The lighter shade could have been thanks to the chemo treatments, but either way, I saw her features when I looked in the mirror more than my dad's. So knowing my clothing would help my dad and I look a little more alike was fine by me.

The letters on my dad's shirt, much like my hoodie, were covered in a thick layer of silver glitter. The only difference was that while his simply announced that he was a cheer dad and had the words "GO MAX" on the back, my hoodie was emblazoned with the TNT Force Logo. It was a logo that covered most of my clothing since joining the cheerleading gym a year and a half ago.

"Okay," I tried again. "Now I'm really ready this time."

After taking my now empty cereal bowl to the sink, I returned to my room for the final trip of the morning to grab my hoodie. I slipped it on then walked to the front door so I could pull on my running shoes. I then made sure to give both of my cats, Thunder and Lightning, a quick scratch under their chins before walking outside to my dad's waiting car. As expected, both of my neighbors were waiting for us to depart.

"Did you sleep in or something?" Peter asked as I moved to climb into the back of the car behind the passenger seat.

"Maybe," I shrugged, then busied myself with settling into the car.

Opening my makeup bag that was sitting in the middle of the back seat, I used the mirror mounted on the back of the headrest in front of me to start getting my face ready for the day. I wouldn't put the last of the glittery and dramatic makeup on until I was getting ready to take the stage and perform. But even still, I wanted to put on at least the base layer of everything so I wouldn't need to spend too much time finishing while I was waiting to cheer.

"This is your last competition before the big one, right?" The question was from Kyle who was climbing into the back seat with me. When I nodded, he continued, "Are you nervous?"

"For this one? No," I said easily, while putting on foundation to help my tan skin look a little darker. "I'm a little nervous about Worlds, but only a little. It's basically like going to Summit last year, just a little bigger. And more important."

"And more people are watching."

The comment came from Peter who had turned around in his seat to join the conversation. Although he was right, I simply went back to putting on my makeup. Usually we had an hour or more in the car, but since we only had a 20-minute drive I knew I needed to work fast. Brushing my short brown hair out of my face, I did the step by step makeup routine I had been performing all season.

Peter and Kyle moved on from the conversation about Worlds, knowing that talking about the international cheerleading competition was clearly a topic I was trying to avoid. Well, that and I really did need to focus on getting ready. Although they were just my neighbors, they were basically my brothers and attended almost all my cheerleading competitions every season. The only ones they missed were the out of town two-day competitions, and of course, they weren't going to be traveling with us for the week-long Worlds tournament in Florida. Although, if they happened to show up suddenly I would only be a little surprised.

"Your phone's buzzing," Kyle announced, holding up my cell for emphasis.

"Anyone important?"

"Just Snapchats from Connor," he replied, then sat my phone back in the cup holder where I had placed it when I loaded into the car.

"You're not going to even see what he sent?" Peter asked, turning in his seat to once again join the conversation.

"I'll check once I'm done with my makeup," I shrugged.

In reply, Peter raised one eyebrow then turned back in his seat to face forward. The facial expression looked so weird on him since he shaved his head. His forehead used to be covered by a fringe of his black hair, but now it was little more than a short stubble covering his head. It made all his expressions more extreme, drawing your focus even more to his green eyes and dark tan skin. Kyle looked the same as Peter; although thankfully he didn't get his hair cut quite as short. It was one of the only things that made it easy to tell the boys apart, especially now that Kyle was starting to get almost as tall as Peter. He was also filling out from conditioning for basketball, making both boys both taller and much more muscular than I was. Or at least muscular in the traditional sense. After all, I could still tumble and fly and dance as well as anyone at the TNT Force gym. All of which took a different kind of strength and muscle.

"Alright, good enough," I said mostly to myself as I began to pack up my makeup a short while later. "How much longer until we get there?"

"About 5 minutes," my dad answered.

Once I finished cramming the rest of my makeup into my glittery teal bag I got to work replying to the many texts and messages that had begun popping up since I got into the car. I replied to a few, then updated my Snapchat story so everyone could see I was about to arrive at the competition. In fact, as I sent the final message out, I looked up to see that we were turning into the small parking lot at the competition arena. Ready or not, it was time to go!

CHAPTER 2

An hour later I stood in front of the stage, waiting with my friends and fellow athletes for Spark to take the floor. The junior level 4 team was performing next, and along with many other athletes, my two best friends were going to be on the mat. Despite the fact that I wasn't performing, I found myself getting nervous. Which was especially odd since I rarely got anxious even when I was about to perform. But still, I could feel the nervousness building until the athletes in the black, white, and orange uniforms took the stage.

"You got this Lexi," I called out as loud as I could once they began finding their starting positions. "Let's go Halley!"

Neither girl responded to me, likely because they couldn't hear me over the roar of others also calling out encouragement. All of that was drowned out a second later when their music began, sending the 32 co-ed athletes into action. Just as they had dozens of times before, each athlete on the mat ran and jumped and cheered, hitting every pose and position just right. Lexi was often high above the mat, lifted by Halley or other bases on the team. She would hold her body in positions she once had to teach me, back when I first joined the gym and entered the world of all-star cheerleading.

The music seemed to reach a crescendo as a voiceover reminded those watching to, "Pay attention now, cuz the Sparks are just starting." Then, in time to a high pitched but familiar sound effect I called out with those around me, the athletes on the mat performed their standing jumps. We yelled hit three times in a row, each yelled as athletes leap off the ground to perform either a toe touch or hurdler. Then, finally, we all yelled pull as each person on the mat performed a back tuck. It was the last of the 'easy' part of the routine, leading into their difficult pyramid and high energy dance. But, as always, they performed like professionals and reached their final pose right on time with the music.

"I didn't see any deductions," Connor said turning to me with a smile.

"Me either," I agreed easily.

I turned then, walking with the crowd of supporters towards where the members of Spark were going to emerge from backstage. Around me, other athletes from my gym also walked with the flow of the crowd, but the group was largely made up of parents whose kids were on Spark. Everyone else from the gym was either in warm-ups or didn't need to be at the competition quite so early. I, along with a few of my friends, on the other hand, always made sure to be there to cheer on Lexi and Halley even if it meant getting to the competition area a few hours early.

"So, what do you think," Connor asked as we stood aside to let parents get a spot closest to the backstage curtain. "Will they keep up their winning streak?"

"Of course," I nodded. "The only other gym in their division barely threw any whips. There's no way Spark will lose to a bunch of back tucks."

The comment was one of many I made every week that gave me pause. They were common enough phrases for me now, but less than two years prior I never would have imagined those words coming out of my own mouth. Not only was I talking about cheerleading, I was talking about it like a seasoned pro. Mostly since, in a way, that's what I was.

After joining the gym on a trial basis, thanks to a bribe from my dad, I entered the

TNT Force Cheer gym at the end of the summer, expecting to be long gone before school even started. But, thanks to amazing friends like Lexi, Halley, and Connor, there were weeks I was at the gym more than I was at home or even school. The place had become a second home for me, especially after winning not one but two first place titles at Summit. It was an international cheerleading competition in Florida that gave me my first real taste of what Worlds might be like. So now, just two weeks until my level 5 team and I would be traveling to the event every cheerleader dreamed of, I was able to easily spout cheer lingo with the best of them.

"How was it?"

Glancing in the directions of the words spoken to me, I was excited to see both Lexi and Halley racing towards me. They were like twins in their matching uniforms, orange cheer bows, and massive smiles. Even their makeup matched, drawing attention to their bright blond hair. Other than the fact that Halley had brown eyes and Lexi had blue, the only real difference between the two was their size. Halley had a good 5 inches on Lexi and had a much more filled out body. She wasn't 'chubby' or 'fat' by anyone's standards but standing next to someone short and thin like Lexi, anyone looked big. Or rather anyone but myself, thanks to her recent growth spurt. Sure, she was only an inch taller than me, but considering she was younger than me I wasn't too thrilled all the same.

"You guys did great!" I announced as my friends both hugged me at the same time. "The pyramid has never looked better."

"Nice tumbling Halley," Connor threw in once the girls were done hugging me and acknowledged him as well.

"Thanks," she grinned, before glancing over her shoulder. "We have to go watch playback. See you guys in a little bit."

With little more than a goodbye, the girls turned and followed their team to where a parent was standing with an iPad. At most competitions, we could watch a replay of our routine in a booth somewhere at the competition site. When one wasn't provided, coaches always made sure the team had something to watch their routine on once they were off the mat. Even though they had hit every part of their routine without a single flaw, it was important to watch it over again in case there were little things they could make even better.

"Well, only 4 hours until we head to warm-ups," Connor said once the athletes from Spark were gone. "What should we do now?"

"Nachos," I said simply.

"Nachos?" he asked.

"Yeah," I nodded. "I smelled them on the way in earlier and if I don't get some I might actually drool on the stage when we perform later."

"We can't have that," Connor said with a laugh. "Nachos it is I guess."

CHAPTER 3

"You seriously smell like nacho cheese," Lexi said with a frown.

"I'm a million percent okay with that," I shrugged. "And thanks. Now that you mentioned it I want more nachos."

Laughing in reply, Lexi went back to drawing on my eyeliner. Even after almost two full seasons of cheerleading, I still struggled to get the winged look just right. Ever since cutting my brown hair into a short inverted bob, a term I only learned after hearing it a few times from my friends and coaches, I was thankfully able to do my own hair. Before getting the help with my makeup, I pulled my hair into a high half ponytail before pinning in my massive teal bow. It would be followed by donning my uniform once my makeup was done and I was ready to head into the warm up room with my team. As usual, I relied on my friends to get the needed products on my face so I would be performance ready.

"What are you going to do when you get to Worlds and we're not there to help with your makeup?" Halley asked.

"You didn't help with my makeup at all today," I pointed out, careful not to move since Lexi was still working on my eyeliner.

"You know what I mean," Halley said with a sigh. "Worlds and Summit are going to be the first time all season we're not together for competition. It's going to be so weird."

"Don't start that now," I warned, opening my eyes to give Halley a warning glance.

"I'm done," she assured me. "No more sad stuff. Let's talk for a second about how tan you look. Are you sure you didn't go to the tanning booth even once?"

"Not even once. I just spent lots of time by the pool."

While Lexi finished my makeup, I was glad to chat about something more casual with my friends. The idea of us not being together for two whole weeks was something we had kind of been ignoring all season. We knew it was coming. Their team couldn't go to Worlds and my team couldn't go to Summit. It was the simple fact of the matter. But even leading up to it all season didn't make it any easier. The one consolation was that we would get to see each other for at least a little bit between the two events. I would make it home in time to see them for a few hours the night before they headed to Florida.

"Alright, time for more nachos," I said, packing up my makeup into my teal glittery bag after slipping on my uniform.

"You were serious?" Halley asked, pausing in applying her lip gloss to look my way.

"Do I ever joke about nachos?"

Knowing the answer was "never" even without me saying it, my friends got up and walked with me to find where my dad was sitting with my backpack and wallet. I checked my phone while we walked, noticing a lot of notifications for the photos I had Halley take while Lexi did my makeup. Thanks to my tumbling videos and general cheer content on my Instagram, I had well over three thousand followers. It was weird at first, but it was quickly becoming one of the many things I had to get used to thanks to my life at the cheer gym. Slipping my phone into the waistband of my uniforms' skirt I was almost to where my dad was sitting when I heard my name being called out.

"Time to go to warm-ups," Connor told me, walking towards me as if he had been looking for me for a while.

"But we don't go back until 5," I reminded him.

"It's 4:53," he replied, holding up his phone for emphasis.

"Oh," I said simply, then turned to my dad. "Watch my phone?"

"Of course," he nodded. "Now get out there and show everyone you're the best cheerleader ever."

His words made me smile and put me into gear as well. I moved forward to hand him my phone and give him a big hug and kiss on the cheek. Then I said goodbye to Peter and Kyle, although they each just got a quick high five from me. Finally, I slipped off my loose fitting black tank top that had been covering the crop top of my uniform. The result was immediate, colors seeming to shimmer around me as the lights in the competition arena sparkled and reflected off the many rhinestones covering the bright fabric. Much more fancy and flashy than my uniforms for the season before, it still took me a second to get used to the disco ball effect it always caused.

As I walked with Connor to where the rest of our squad was waiting, I tugged on the hem of the cropped top to ensure it was sitting just right. The bright teal and black fabric were eye catching and allowed the embroidered letters of Nitro across the chest to stand out perfectly. But, my favorite part was that the uniform had a small pop of lime green in it as well. Designed to help all the TNT Force level 5 teams feel like one unit, each teams' uniform featured a little of another squad's signature color. Bomb Squad had a little of Nitro's teal on their uniform, Nitro had some lime green to represent Detonators, and Detonators had a hint of hot pink for Bomb Squad. It was nice to know even that when we were on stage we had our fellow gym mates with us up there in a small way.

"Ready to kill it Max?" TJ, my coach, asked once I was standing with my team members who were slowly walking into the warmup room.

"You know it," I grinned, giving him a high-five.

"Good," he said in reply. "Start warming up."

His final comment wasn't just to me, but rather to all the athletes around me. We got into our usual formation to begin our jumping jacks, kicks, and other basic warm ups. The movements were all sharp and angular, but second nature to myself and the 19 athletes around me. Most of what we were about to do was all second nature. Like every competition all season we would warm up with conditioning, then tumbling, and finally stunts. Then, once we were called onto the stage, we would perform through the two and a half minutes of choreography we had long since memorized. The only wild card was whether we would perform perfectly or if we would make mistakes along the way. Sure, it didn't matter too much since we would be performing at Worlds either way. But, we still wanted to head to Florida after another first place. It would set the stage for the moment we had been waiting for all season. All the wins would almost feel like they were for nothing if we walked away from Worlds without a 1st place trophy like Nitro and the TNT Force Worlds teams had in the past. Everyone agreed it was finally time for Nitro to hold that honor.

CHAPTER 4

As the music pumping through the sound system changed for our upbeat dance sequence, I spun around once before turning and making my way to the back of the stage. Counting the music in my head I moved my arms in the detailed choreography for two counts of eight before walking to where Matthew, Connor, and Juleah were all waiting for me. Stepping up to stand in their arms I took in a deep breath and was then launched into the air. I flew quickly thanks to their added momentum, then began to fall back to the earth almost immediately. Knowing I had no time to waste, I kicked my leg up as high as I could before spinning my body around twice as I returned to the arms of my teammates.

They held me for a few seconds, then as the crowd began to cheer and scream, set me back on my feet. Everyone around me also unfroze from their final pose, a spot they reached on the same beat that I landed with my stunt team. It made for a dynamic finish that kept the crowd entertained until the last second. I tried to see if my dad was holding up a thumbs up to show me we hit the routine perfectly, but couldn't see him as Connor wrapped his arms around me and picked me up for a massive hug.

"Did we hit?" I asked, desperate to know if we managed to once again perform a routine free of any and all deductions.

"Yes," he replied while spinning me around once before setting me back on my feet.

Knowing we needed to clear the stage, I started to head off the blue mat while also looking for Emma. Spotting her small frame and curly blond hair as we reached the edge of the stage, I linked my arm with hers as we continued walking. The speakers in the area were once again pumping out loud music to keep those in attendance of the competition entertained while they waited for the next team to take the stage. It made it impossible to talk, so I waited until we were past the speakers and walking through the exit to the backstage before I tried to speak.

"Did you hit your bow and arrow?"

"Yup," she grinned, then paused in walking to hug me. "Did you try the kick-kick?"

"Not this time," I said with a shake of my head. "But I think I had the height for it. Maybe I can debut it at Worlds."

"Good plan," she nodded as we continued our progress.

We walked down the long hallway backstage that led to the athlete's exit where our friends and family were waiting. Most importantly, TJ was also there, a grin covering his face. There were hugs and celebrating all around me, my dad giving me the longest and tightest hug of them all. It was all a blur as we accepted the congratulations while also making our way to where Halley's mom was standing with an iPad for us to re-watch the performance. Once we all reached her our coach spoke to us before hitting play.

"Today was exactly how we want to end the season," he grinned. "I couldn't be prouder of you and the performance you just gave. We still have some tough competition coming up at Worlds, but after today I'm not worried. As long as you kids stay healthy and do in Florida what you just did out there, then I'm confident it's going to be our best year yet."

A few athletes cheered and clapped in agreement, but I simply watched TJ with a smile on my face. I had known TJ since I first joined the gym, and even when he wasn't my coach I always looked up to him. He was built like the other guys in the gym, tall and muscular from years of tumbling and lifting girls into the air. Despite being at least twice my age, TJ still looked much younger thanks to his blond hair that was still dyed teal in the front. The color brought out his bright blue eyes that were surrounded by crow's feet and age lines that were just starting to show his age. What I really focused on in that moment though was the grin spread across his face. Even after winning competitions all season, the look on his face was somehow filled with more excitement and pride than ever before.

"You totally could have done the kick-kick," Emma said, bringing my focus back to the iPad that was showing the end of the routine.

"Your basket at the start looked pretty amazing," I replied, although I hadn't actually watched the replay.

"The whole routine looked great," she said simply.

I nodded in reply, not wanting to admit I hadn't seen the video. It seemed to be enough though, since Emma began going on and on again talking about the elite stunt section and the standing jumps. All of it really did go perfectly, not a single mistake or point deduction along the way. Or at least that was what I could assume after listening to her talk about it as we slowly made our way to where our bags, parents, and the rest of the TNT athletes were waiting. We arrived in a sea of people wearing familiar team colors and lots of rhinestones. But somehow, through it all, I found Lexi and Halley easily.

"Okay," I said to both of them as I reached into my backpack to find my phone. "We're getting nachos now, right?"

"Seriously?"

The question was from Halley. She was wearing an orange tank top over her uniform, the word TNT Force spelled out in bright silver and black glitter. Seeing it reminded me of my own tank top, so I quickly dug it out of my bag and slipped it on over my uniform. Once it was in place I glanced at my phone. I ignored the many notifications that were showing on my lock screen, and instead looked at the time. Seeing we had less than twenty minutes before the final award session of the day, I knew going in search of food would have to wait for a while. It might have meant no more nachos, but I knew winning first place would more than make up for it.

"Nachos later," I told both Halley and Lexi. "How about we go pick out a bow instead."

Glad to continue our tradition from last season, my friends flashed me big smiles before searching for their wallets. When we were on Blast together we would buy bows

29

when we lost to help make up for the sadness that went with not landing in the top spot. But, considering losses were few and far between now that I was on Nitro and my friends were on Spark, we simply bought bows to continue to add to our collections. And, as much as I hated to admit it, the super glittery bows were growing on me.

"I saw the perfect one earlier," Lexi announced, then led the charge to the many merchandise tables covered in bows.

CHAPTER 5

"Can you please tell Max she needs to try the kick-kick," Emma whined to TJ on Monday afternoon as we met in the gym for Nitro team practice.

"We won Saturday with just the kick double," I reminded her. I was still feeling pretty pumped up thanks to our first-place win, coming in first of the level 5 teams at the event, and getting the top score of the whole competition.

"She has a point, though," TJ said with a nod. "We're going to be going up against the same teams we faced at NCA. And as much as we've improved since then, I'm certain they have as well."

His words weren't what I wanted to hear at that moment, but they were true all the same. The National Cheerleading Association competition in Dallas earlier in the season was the first time we got to compete against the teams we would be facing at Worlds. Even thinking about that weekend was a sore subject, considering we hit a perfect routine but still ended up in 5th place. Like TJ said, we had made changes in the routine to make it harder and to raise our raw score potential. But, also like he said, everyone else we competed against had been making changes as well. It was impossible to go on YouTube most weekends without seeing the big gyms posting their polished and even more difficult routines. All of it raised the bar to an even higher level that we had to make sure we could reach as well.

"I'm willing to try it I guess," I finally said, hoping that agreeing to try the flying skill would end the conversation.

"Perfect," TJ said immediately. "Let's try it now before we start conditioning."

"Right now?" I asked in clarification, certain I had heard him wrong.

"No time like the present," he grinned.

Despite the fact that Nitro team practice didn't start for another half an hour, most of the members of the team had already arrived to get in extra work before practice, or at the very least to hang out before we got down to serious business and hard work. Hoping to get it over with, I hopped up onto my feet and moved to stand on the center of the mat. It was one of four spring loaded floors that ran along the length of the gym. I stood to face the mirrored wall, wanting to see as much of the basket toss I was about to try as possible.

Emma, who had been sitting next to me a moment before, moved towards the edge of the mat to sit and watch with a few of the other fliers on the team. Once they realized what was going on, a few more people joined them, threatening my willingness to give the difficult flying skill a try. But, I knew I couldn't back out as Matthew, Connor, and Juleah all moved to stand with me. Juleah wasn't as tall as the boys, but since she was my back spot of the stunt it didn't matter as much when it came to holding me and tossing me up.

What did matter was that both Matthew and Connor were over 6 feet tall and had muscles built for throwing girls into the air. Matthew had a serious expression on his face, his angular jaw adding to the look. It was the face he made when focusing, something I saw Lexi, his sister, make often as well. The look was even more intense thanks to his white blond hair, bright blue eyes, and the thin layer of stubble that was noticeable on his chin. When the serious look on his face was too much, I glanced at Connor and instantly felt much more at ease. Connor was smiling at me, his dimples easy to spot across the whole room. The expression helped to calm my nerves, making me glad to have my best friend there to catch me, not to mention toss me as well. Running a hand through his curly black hair, Connor locked his green eyes on mine and simply asked: "Ready?"

I nodded in reply, not trusting myself to talk. Something about trying a skill I had only worked on a few times, now with so many people from my squad watching and probably filming, was making me strangely uneasy. I knew if I messed up or failed at all they wouldn't be disappointed, but it would make me feel like I let them down all the same. Pushing those thoughts aside, I followed TJ's instructions and got ready for the basket toss. He only wanted me to do a kick double to start so we easily obliged, the stunt team throwing and catching me easily.

"You have more than enough height," TJ said to me once my feet were back on the mat. "But let's work up to it just in case. This time do a kick single, then just another kick. No twist on the second one."

I was once again tossed in the air, following his instructions easily. Kicking my left leg as high as I could while also reaching up my left arm to touch my toes, I snapped my leg back down and began a full rotation of my body. Once I knew the ground was once again under me as it had been for the first kick, I completed the kick again, this time preparing to be caught after my legs were together. Bracing myself for the slightly jarring feeling of being caught, I was surprised how much time seemed to pass between the kick and landing in the arms of the athletes below me.

"Was I really that high?" I asked instantly.

"Yes," Emma called out to me from her spot on the mat. "If it was legal you could almost do a kick single-kick double."

"Let's just stick to the legal move," Connor said simply. He still had a hand on my shoulder and gave it a gentle squeeze of encouragement. "Don't worry Max, we won't let you fall."

The truth was I was going to fall. I was literally going to be thrown up into the air and then would start falling immediately. But, the important thing was that I would need to work hard to twist and spin to be in the right position to be caught before I was done with the falling. Hopefully, it would keep me from slipping out of their grip and in doing so make contact with the floor under me. Despite its springs, landing on the mat was never a nice feeling.

"Here we go," TJ finally said, then counted us into the stunt.

Performing almost the same moves as just moments before I added the full twist in after the second kick easily. The landing, however, was a little harder than I was expecting it to be. I knew I would likely have a bruise on my underarms thanks to how I was caught. Or at least, I knew I would after the next few attempts I was certain were still to come.

"Not bad Max," TJ said with a big grin, talking over the athletes that were actually clapping at the basket toss. "This time really think about how you're coming in for the landing."

"Got it," I said simply, then got ready to try the skill once again. And again. And again. In the end, we tried the same basket toss over 10 times, each time the move becoming easier to land. Much like the other skills I had learned since joining the gym, once my muscles got used to the movements, it became second nature. By the time we were done I could actually see the start of a bruise on my left arm, but knew I would need to simply deal with it for a while. Especially since despite the hard work I had just put in to learn the kick-full-kick-full, practice was just getting started.

CHAPTER 6

"What happened now?" Peter asked Tuesday afternoon, pointing to the large bruise on my left arm.

"Cheer." I paused then continued. "Like always."

"Well yeah, I figured that," he laughed. "I mean what happened exactly."

"My stunt team and I tried a new skill," I explained. "We want to make the kick double at the very end of the routine a kick-single-kick-single. But it means me getting more air so I'm landing a little harder. I think the bruise wouldn't have shown up at all if it wasn't for the very first one we tried. And it was totally my fault. I wasn't thinking about landing after just doing a single around instead of a double around."

Peter nodded, and I was instantly thankful for a best friend that was interested in what I did in my free time. When I first joined the gym, I didn't even tell him or Kyle for a while, certain they would make fun of me. Sure, they thought it was kind of lame for a while, but once they saw just what I was doing, they were super supportive. So much so that Peter was spending his Tuesday night helping me get ahead in math since I was going to be missing almost a full week of school for Worlds. We were sitting at my kitchen table with an assortment of books and papers all around us. Peter was two years ahead of me in school, so he was a great person to get help from until my dad arrived home from work.

"Just don't get hurt for real so close to Worlds," he said simply, then went back to explaining the problem we were working on before he had noticed my bruise.

"I won't," I assured him.

As we went back to work I could hear my phone chiming over and over again from where it was sitting on the kitchen counter. I had it plugged in to charge for a while, and picked a spot across the room so I wouldn't get too distracted while doing homework. The only problem with that was that the text tone was almost just as distracting as actually reading messages. I tried to block it out for a while, but in the end, I knew I had to see what was going on before I could actually get more work done.

"Let me guess, it's Lexi," Peter said when I began laughing at the messages I was pulling up on my phone.

"Nope," I said with a shake of my head. "Just Connor."

At my words, I watched as Peter clenched his jaw and look away from me and back down at the paper in front of him. Assuming he was annoyed at the distraction, I quickly sent a few Snapchat messages to Connor in reply to his photos then turned my phone to silent. I knew there would likely be a lot more messages coming in since it appeared Connor was at the gym and learning the dance portion of Bomb Squads' routine. As an all-girl squad, the dancing was a lot flashier and sassier than anything the boys on Nitro performed. I wasn't sure exactly why Connor was learning the dance considering he hadn't even told me he was going to the gym at all, but it made me instantly want to grab my bike and head across town to join him. Despite having practice three times a week, I often found myself wishing I could be at the gym even more. Knowing Peter wouldn't be happy if I blew off our homework session for even more cheer, I simply returned to the table to get back to work.

"Are people at the gym allowed to date?"

"What?" I asked, Peter's question catching me completely off guard.

"Do the coaches or the gym or whatever have a rule about whether athletes are allowed to date one another?" he clarified.

"I don't think so," I began slowly, still confused as to why Peter was bringing up the subject. "Actually, there can't be. Emma and Matthew have been dating for a really long time now, and I want to say there is at least one couple on Detonators. Why?"

"No reason." Peter was clearly lying, and when he saw my raised eyebrows he decided to try again. "I was just thinking it would be really stupid for athletes to date someone at the gym since it could be a really big distraction."

"That makes sense," I nodded. "But I feel like we're all mature enough to not let it be an issue. I mean, you would never be able to tell Matthew and Emma were together during practice if you didn't already know. They focus on what they have to do and everything way too much to let something like their relationship get in the way of cheer."

"What if they get in a fight or break up?" Peter challenged.

"That wouldn't matter," I said, although I was just guessing. "Everyone is so focused on the team and what's important that they would never let anything get in the way of working hard. I mean, some of us are at the gym 4 and 5 times a week, so we would never let something silly like a boyfriend get in the way of our goals."

"Okay," he said simply, although something about his tone seemed off still.

"Why did you want to know?" I asked. I set down my pencil as if to let him know I wasn't going to get back to work until I had a real answer.

"When you were talking to Connor I was just thinking that you're on a team that actually has guys and girls," he began slowly. "I haven't been on a co-ed team for sports since I was on my kindergarten soccer team. I just figured it must be a little strange since at our age people start to date, so it would make sense for the gym to have a rule in place to keep it to a minimum or something."

The whole time Peter was speaking he refused to make eye contact with me. Instead, he held his pen in his hand, flicking it just right to make it spin around his thumb and allowing him to catch it only to repeat the move again and again. It was something I couldn't quite master, despite Peter trying to teach me a few times. He didn't do the trick around me much thanks to my annoyance at not being able to replicate it, so the fact he was suddenly trying it over and over made me think he was using it as a distraction. What he was trying to distract himself from was a mystery. A mystery that would have to wait for another time.

"Alright," I finally said with a sigh. "Back to work. There's no way I'm saving any of this for when I get to Florida."

CHAPTER 7

"This is bad," Juleah sighed, pausing the video that had been playing on her phone.

"What's bad?" I asked, sitting down next to her on the blue mat to begin stretching.

"My friend Jill that cheers up in Tulsa hurt her hip yesterday," she explained, handing me her phone to watch the video. "She's out for Worlds, and who knows how long past that."

Taking the phone from Juleah I watched as the athlete that must have been Jill run across a mat in her gym for a tumbling pass. I watched as she performed a basic round off, followed by two back handsprings. She ended the pass with a full, which was a backflip with the addition of a full twist. It was a move I could do in my sleep, and it appeared Jill was also quite good at the skill as well. But, once she landed she seemed to have more bounce than she expected. She was thrown off balance, taking first one step backward, then another. The steps took her off the edge of the gym mat and caused her to trip on the concrete floor that was suddenly underneath her feet. I watched in shock and almost horror as her body turned slightly as she fell, causing her hip to crash into the hard floor.

"Oh my goodness," I said slowly, instantly imagining just how she must have felt. Not only would a landing like that hurt you, as Juleah explained that it had, but missing the rest of the cheer season because of it was sure to be just as big of a blow. "I can't image what she's going through."

"Her doctor said she might need to have surgery to fix it," Juleah explained, taking her phone from me and setting it face down on the mat. "She's mostly just worried about Worlds. Her team's going to have a hard time replacing her. And she's not sure if she can even be there to watch if they perform without her."

"Has she been to Worlds before?"

"Nope, not yet," Juleah said with a frown.

I listened as she explained that Jill used to cheer for TNT Force before she moved to Oklahoma two years before I joined the gym. Her gym didn't compete at the same locations we did very often, so Worlds was going to be the first time Juleah would get to see her since her team skipped out on nationals. I could tell even talking about it all was making Juleah antsy. While she spoke, she pulled her wavy red hair out of its ponytail only to put it back up again complete with our Nitro team practice bows. During the chat, she kept her blue eyes locked on the mat, likely still replaying the video repeatedly like I was as well.

"Hopefully she'll be back up and running in no time," I said hopefully. "And maybe she'll luck out and can make it to Worlds to at least watch so you can still see her."

"Hopefully," Juleah agreed.

As we began warmups a few minutes later I couldn't get the image from the video out of my head. Sure, seeing Jill hit the ground was hard to watch, but seeing the look on her face in agony was much more haunting. I think it was likely because her face was in agony over not just the injury but likely also what the injury meant. All of it also made me think of when Cassidy got injured, which allowed me to perform with Fuze at Summit less than a year ago. The idea of working all year just to have it taken away so close to the end of the season seemed like the worst possible thing that could happen to a cheerleader.

"You doing okay?" Matthew asked as we lined up to run the whole routine for the first time that evening. It was after our standard conditioning and other warm ups.

"What?" I asked, having not actually heard what he said.

"Are you okay?" he tried again. "I can tell you're thinking about something else."

"No," I said with a shake of my head. "I mean yes. I'm fine. And yes, I'm thinking about something else, but I'm going to be okay. Really."

"So, what is it that has you so distracted?" He hooked a thumb to point over to Connor who was watching me from his place on the mat. When Matthew made eye contact with me again he had a strange smile on his face.

"I get it, everyone can tell," I said with a sigh. "I'm just worried about getting hurt. What if I get injured and ruin everything when we're finally almost there."

"That's what not I meant, I- Never mind," Matthew mumbled, giving his head a shake. "You need to stop worrying though. If you focus on getting hurt, you'll make mistakes and really will get hurt. Or, at the very least you'll make mistakes all the time. You need to focus on right here and right now. Time to kill it, okay?"

I knew Matthew was right. Even though he was Lexi's older brother, he was like a brother to me as well. Not just because he was my stunt partner but also because he was always there to look out for me. It could have been because I was the youngest person on the team, the shortest person by quite a few inches, and one of the newest team members. Whatever the reason, I was beyond thankful to have him as a teammate for the season. It was also going to be his last season, something I wasn't quite ready to think about until after Worlds was over.

"Okay," I finally said. "Let's kill it."

Minutes later as TJ finally started our music and we began our first run through, or full out, of the night, I did what Matthew said. I tried to focus on the skills and choreography I had spent all season perfecting, trying my hardest to make sure everything went as planned. Despite a few minor errors like spinning right instead of left during the first eight count of the dance sequence, and trying a kick single instead of a kick double during my major tumbling pass, everything went as planned. Or at least it went as planned for me. Based on TJ's comments once we finished the routine I knew there were other errors on the mat.

"That better have been a warm up," he called out in obvious frustration. "You shouldn't even be tired yet, so there's no excuse. Let's go again."

Moving to my spot for the opening of the routine, I reminded myself I needed to hit everything perfectly. Watering down my tumbling or even messing up while dancing wasn't good enough so late in the season. So, I once again pushed myself as hard as I could, trying to run the whole routine without a mistake. When my tumbling pass came, I took an extra deep breath, then allowed my muscle memory to take over.

Running a few steps to gain power, I slammed my feet down and flipped forward in what is known as a punch front. When my feet hit the ground, I turned my body around as I flipped, all while also twisting in the air to land facing the direction I had just come from. The move was an Arabian and allowed me to transition into a round off followed by a back hand spring then a whip. For the whip, I performed a basic backflip but kept my entire body straight while doing so. When my feet made contact with the mat, I once again flipped my body around, this time adding in a full twisting motion. It slowed me down a little, as usual, so I added in one more back handspring before trying my final move.

Kicking my leg up while also reaching up a hand to touch my toes, I performed a backflip while twisting not once but twice. The skill was commonly known as a kick double and was the hardest part of my tumbling pass. It was also great on the score sheets, especially when I followed the move with another punch front so I could continue to the center of the mat. This second punch front led into a more basic round off followed by a back hand spring and yet another kick double. It left me tired, to say the least, but I had no time to rest. Instead, I used the bouncing momentum after the last tumbling skill to hop into the hands of my stunt team that was waiting for me at the center of the mat. They easily picked me up, spinning me around twice on my way to being held high above their heads. Happy to have landed my hard tumbling sequence, the grin on my face was genuine as I moved to continue with the rest of the routine.

CHAPTER 8

"Is it too early to start packing?" I asked Halley and Lexi on Thursday evening as we sat in my room. We were surrounded by magazines as we looked for the perfect outfits to wear to the end of the year banquet in a few more weeks. I was less interested than my friends were in finding a dress, my mind spending more and more time focused on Worlds.

"No," Lexi said with the shake of her head. "If anything, it's better that way. Then you won't forget anything."

I thought about it for a few minutes, then decided not to pack just yet. Mostly because I didn't want to ruin one of the last times I would get to hang out with my two best friends before leaving for Florida.

Although their team would be practicing on the mat next to Nitro once before I left for Worlds, I knew there wouldn't really be time to hang out while in the gym since my focus would be on practice instead. My weekend would be filled with getting ready to leave, which included a day out with Tonya. And finally, after two long practices on Monday and Tuesday nights, I would board a plane bright and early Wednesday morning to fly to Orlando. It was a moment I had been waiting for since we got our Worlds bid in January, although it was just finally starting to feel like it was real, so to speak.

"I think I want to get a gold dress," Lexi said, pointing to something a celebrity was wearing on the red carpet in one of the pages in front of her.

"What if we don't win gold at Summit though?" Halley challenged.

"Good point," she said with a sigh.

"Or you could still wear gold since it was a great season," I suggested. "I mean, you guys have won first at almost every competition. To me, the whole season is just as important as the final performance."

"Well yeah," Lexi began slowly. "But I really want to win Summit again."

We all easily agreed, then launched into talking about how much fun we had at Summit just under a year ago. It was the first competition all season where we got to be in the same hotel room for the week, and it

made for a lot of late nights and craziness.
Even with parents on the other side of the
door in their connected room, we were able
to hang out and feel more like adults. Sure,
we were still kids by all standards, but it was
fun all the same.

"Do you know who you get to room
with at Worlds?" Lexi asked once we were
done laughing about swimming all night after
the final awards last year.

"I think Emma, Juleah, and Addison,
but I'm not sure," I explained. "There was
also talk about some of us rooming with
people from Bomb Squad or Detonators too,
so it might change. We have so many
practices going on while we're there though, I
don't really think it will matter much."

"Yeah, but it will be worth it when you
win it all," Halley reminded me.

"You mean if we win it all," I replied
instantly.

"You're doing a kick-single-kick-single
now, right?" When I nodded, Halley
continued. "That's a major move. With lots of
points. Not to mention you have your kick
double in your tumbling passes and everyone
on the team is throwing at least a full or
double full. I don't think Nitro has ever looked
this good. It's your year to win it for sure as
long as everyone hits the routine and no one
gets hurt."

"Fingers crossed," I said simply, then
went back to looking at the magazines.

The truth was, I felt like it was our year as well. It was well known in the cheer world that TNT Force had never won a Worlds title. Or a Summit title for that matter. Well, at least until last season. For some reason, it was like no matter how many times the teams won all season, something would go wrong at Worlds. They would drop a stunt or miss a tumbling pass. Just a big enough error to miss out on the coveted Worlds rings that the first place teams took home. And sure, winning second was great. But no amount of second place trophies could ever compare to winning first just once.

When my phone buzzed next to me, I was glad for the distraction. Seeing the message was from Connor, I replied immediately, happy to talk about our final team practices. Thanks to the athletes on Nitro begging and pleading all season we were making the final three practices leading into Worlds dress up nights. Friday we were planning to wear special shirts a mom from the gym had printed for us, Monday was a Disney character dress up, but Tuesday was all about camouflage.

We were all planning to wear camo since we were 'ready for war' once we got to Worlds. The three days were something we had been planning for a while, so we had outfits ready to go. But, as it always seemed to happen with theme nights for Nitro team practice, Emma wanted to add more items last minutes. According to the messages from Connor, he ran into Emma at the store and she was buying face paint and black lipstick for Tuesday so everyone would look even more intense. His warning helped me be prepared with a forced smile when Emma sent me a few Snapchats a minute later.

"What's he saying now?" Halley asked, watching me take a selfie to send to Emma.

"What?" I asked, instantly confused.

"You're talking to Connor, right?"

"Kind of," I said as I sent the message. "That one was to Emma though. She wants us to wear black lipstick and face paint Tuesday on top of our camo. Connor warned me just before Emma gave me the news."

"He warned you?" Lexi asked. "Why would he need to warn you of something so fun?"

"I hate wearing makeup to the gym," I explained simply. "So, if we're getting special lipstick and all that then everyone else is going to be all fancy. That means I either have to do it too or stand out for not taking part."

"Or you just use more face paint to look cool," Halley tried. "Everyone knows you're not a girly-girl. It's what people love about you. You don't need to go all out with makeup if you don't want to. Emma will totally understand."

"I hope so," I nodded, then typed a message to Connor. I knew my friends were watching from their spots next to me on my bed, but I didn't mind. We didn't have secrets or anything like that between us, so if they read what I explained to Connor, that I wasn't going to go all out with my makeup, it didn't bother me. Or at least not until they started making comments.

"Do you think Connor will be sad you don't get dressed up?" Lexi asked.

"No way," Halley said before I could speak. "He totally doesn't care about that."

"Right," I nodded, although their words left me confused. "If you two don't care if I wear makeup or not, there's no way Connor would either."

My two friends shared a look then let out a giggle. It was something they did often enough that I was able to ignore them as I exited my Snapchat app to open Instagram. As always, there were hundreds of notifications to go through before glancing at the main feed. Ever since I joined Nitro, people seemed a lot more interested in following my cheerleading career online. It was largely thanks to Leanne, a former teammate of mine that chose to post terrible things about me to the social media app. The cyber bullying caused her removal from the gym, and in the end turned out to be a positive thing. There were a lot of people who told me they looked up to me and were inspired by how I didn't let her bully me and instead stood up for myself. There were also a lot of cheer companies that began contacting me for promotions. At least once a month I got items in the mail that I would post photos of in exchange for the free products. It was a little overwhelming at times, but I got to share the items with my friends so that made it a little more fun.

"I haven't done a tumbling video in a while," I said absentmindedly as I went through my own photos to read the latest comments from my followers.

"We could go play on your air mat for a while," Lexi suggested. "We could even do a live video if you want."

"Sure," I said simply, easily setting the magazines aside. "Maybe you can finally land your full, Halley."

"Don't count on it," she laughed, then stood up to head outside.

CHAPTER 9

Watching Halley flip and fly through the air, I called out encouragements as she reached the end of the mat. She performed two back handsprings, using her hands and the backflip to gain momentum and get additional height. Then, just before she would run right off the mat she began a final backflip, while also turning her body in a full twist before landing on her feet. The landing was a bit messy, with two steps backward off the mat. But, it was her best attempt yet, something both Lexi and I instantly celebrated.

"You did it!" Lexi exclaimed, jumping up to hug Halley.

"Kind of," she replied, although she had a massive smile covering her face.

"Kind of counts," I added. "That was still awesome, and I bet by the time we get to assessments for next season you can land it on the blue mat."

"Then maybe we can all be on Nitro together!" Lexi jumped up and down as she yelled this, clearly excited at just the thought of us all being on the same team for another season.

Although I didn't show my excitement by jumping up and down like Lexi, the thought of getting to be on a team with my best friends once again was amazing. I had made a lot of friends on Nitro, but Lexi and Halley were the ones who first got me interested in cheerleading. I first met them at our local indoor trampoline park after seeing their flips and skills and went over to talk to them. Then we chatted and they taught me their tricks. After that, they invited me to an open gym, and the rest is history. I spent my whole first season of cheer on the mat with Lexi and Halley, with Halley as my back spot for all my flying skills. Even when I was on Fuze, a senior level 4 team, for a few weeks, Blast was still where I felt most at home. Sure, I couldn't do the harder skills from Nitro like fulls and double arounds when performing on the junior level 3 team, but having my best friends there for me every time I took the mat was more than worth it.

"Okay, I need a break," Halley announced, moving to find her water bottle.

"Max's turn," Lexi called out. She sat down where she and I had been sitting just before to watch Halley.

With a shrug, I moved away from them, getting a few running steps before launching into a round off followed by a back handspring and then a double full. Each movement was one I could do in my sleep, so it took little effort. I knew it would have still been easy if I added in the kick motion to the double full rotation, but didn't want to 'show off' too much. Or at least that was my plan until my friends started encouraging me to do more. They were filming with my phone, likely uploading everything straight to Instagram thanks to the live feature. Wanting to make entertaining content for the dozens of people I knew might be watching, I gave in easily and worked on more skills.

"Okay, I think I'm done," I said to Lexi, Halley, and the camera after doing a few more running tumbling passes.

"Fine," Lexi said with a frown.

"Wait," Halley quickly added. "You have to end with something awesome. You should try a kick triple or a standing double."

"I don't think I can land those even if I wanted to," I said simply while walking to set up one final time. "I have another idea."

I was tired, my body feeling the muscle strain of working for so long. But I knew I should still try to end with something amazing. So, despite feeling like my legs were turning to jelly, and my arms weren't strong enough for even one more round off, I got set up for more. There had been enough times during competition and even practice that I was forced to push through fatigue, so I was determined to do so once again.

Giving my friends and the cameras a nod, I took three running steps before launching onto the air mat and into the moves I was planning. The air mat allowed me to get extra height off the ground, so I quickly threw my body forward in a front flip, or punch front. Once my feet were on the ground I performed a round off so my body was in the right position for the rest of the moves I had planned. Pushing with my legs, I flipped over, twisting once to execute a full. As soon as my feet landed, I pushed off again, performing the skill a second time, only with an added twist. The double full was easy enough for me, even with how tired I was. But it wasn't the end of the tumbling pass just yet.

Using all my strength to push off the ground one final time, I flipped in the air, kicking my leg up as I went. Once my leg was as high as it could go, I snapped it down while rotating my body twice. The resulting kick double full was something I did enough while on the mat with Nitro that it was usually easy to accomplish. Thanks to the full and double full I had thrown leading into the kick double, however, I knew before my feet landed that something was wrong. With the ground rushing up to meet my body, I could tell I wasn't going to be able to plant my toes like usual. There was nothing I could about it though, so I simply prepared myself to fall either forward or backward after gravity finally set me down.

The second my feet met the mat I could feel a sharp pain in my right ankle, the feeling eliciting a yelp from my mouth. As I tucked and rolled my body in a kind of somersault to lessen the fall onto the grass at the end of the mat, I remembered my friends were watching as well as filming. So, doing my best to play off the fall and also the pain that was coursing through my leg, I started laughing. Glancing towards Halley and Lexi I watched their shocked and worried faces turn to smiles. They stopped filming and headed my way, laughing with me and congratulating me on the attempted tumbling pass.

"That was awesome," Lexi grinned.

"I didn't land it though," I said, smashing my teeth together in my best attempt at a smile and in an effort to ignore the pain in my ankle. "I think I'm about done for a while."

"Yeah," Halley nodded. "We should head inside. Sitting in the grass is getting cold."

"And I'm getting hungry," Lexi announced.

"I'm sure my dad's already cooking dinner. You guys can stay if you want."

While my friends agreed, and picked up their water bottles, I grabbed the airmat and began walking inside. I kept a smile on my face as I chatted with my friends about what food we wanted the most, dragging the lightweight mat with me as I walked. But on the inside, I knew something was wrong. My right ankle was hurting, sending a shooting pain up my leg and through my foot every time I applied weight to it. With my brain reminding myself over and over again that I was leaving for Worlds in just a few days, I ignored the pain, praying it would go away after a good night's sleep.

CHAPTER 10

"Ready to go?" my dad asked as I walked out of my room Friday afternoon.

I nodded, quickly grabbing my backpack and slipping it on over my new team gear. The baseball style shirt had black sleeves and a teal front with "Ready For Worlds" written in glittery letters. The TNT logo was hidden in the swirls and bursts around the words, which was a fun detail most of us didn't notice until it was pointed out. On the back, we each had our last names and the year. So, mine simply read "TURNER" with a 17 underneath. Much like the front, this was done with glittery letters that were easy to spot from even far away. I finished the look with my black shorts, as usual, resisting the urge to also add an ace bandage to my ankle for good measure.

After Lexi and Halley left, I told my dad I was tired and going to do homework before bed. The truth was my ankle was hurting even worse. By the time I took a look at it I realized it was also quite swollen. Once I was certain my dad was sitting in the living room watching his evening shows, I snuck into the kitchen for ice. I grabbed a Popsicle as well to cover my reason for going into the freezer, but considering my dad never even looked my way, I was in the clear even without the decoy treat.

The ice felt nice, and taking some ibuprofen that I had stashed in my cheer bag also seemed to take some of the sting away. What was concerning, however, was that it didn't take away all of the pain, just seemed to lessen it a little. Even after elevating it while I worked on homework, and then trying to stay off of it for most of the day at school, it was still hurting. Not as much as when it first happened, but something was wrong all the same. Knowing wrapping it would draw attention to the injury, I gave myself the mental reminder to ignore it and push through the pain. It would be hard during tumbling and certain stunts, but it was worth the risk if it would keep TJ from finding out and make me miss performing at Worlds.

"You doing okay Max?"

"What?" I asked in reply. I had been staring out the window as we drove across town to the gym, and had clearly been wrapped up in my thoughts.

"I asked if you're doing okay," my dad tried again, giving me a concerned look as he spoke.

"Yeah," I said weakly. "I'm just focused on practice. Only a few left before Worlds."

"Don't stress too much honey." I watched his face relax, clearly believing my excuse. "Just take it one day at a time. You kids are all ready, you just have to work together and stay calm. I know you can do it Max. As good as Blast and Fuze were last season going into Summit, Nitro is even more prepared by a long shot."

"Thanks Dad," I smiled, truly thankful for his comment. Even though I was more worried about my ankle than how the whole team would perform, just hearing his confidence in me and the other athletes on Nitro was still pretty great.

Once we arrived, I said goodbye to my dad and watched him walk into the room next to the office while I walked into the gym. It was filled with the other parents who were planning to watch their children during practice. Spark and Blast were both working on the mats closest to the door, so I gave a quick wave to Lexi and Halley before walking to the far mat where Nitro was stretching and getting ready for practice. As I walked, I made sure to keep a straight face, not letting the pain I was feeling show. It was a rather dull throb, so I was able to ignore it most of the time without much thought. I knew once Nitro practice was in full swing, ignoring it might not be so easy. With that in mind, I went straight to Matthew to act on something I had been thinking through all day.

"Can I talk to you for a minute?" I asked him, an eager look on my face.

"What's up?" Matthew spoke casually, then took in my expression. "Is everything okay?"

"Yeah," I shrugged. "Can we go over there?"

Matthew simply nodded then followed me away from the rest of our team and closer to the wall of mirrors. Thankfully only Emma had been standing within earshot when I spoke to Matthew, and she appeared to be distracted while texting someone. I knew it wouldn't be long until Emma realized I was talking to Matthew and wanting to join the conversation. So I spoke quickly, making sure to give Matthew as much information as he needed to keep me safe while still downplaying my injury as much as possible.

"So, I kind of hurt myself," I said, then rushed on before he could reply. "I like tweaked my ankle, but it was basically nothing. It doesn't really hurt anymore but like kind of does sometimes. But it's like not really a big thing. And I think I'll be fine. But I wanted to like tell you about it so you knew. Since you could like maybe make sure with my flying I'm like okay and all that? I think I'll be okay to tumble though. Like, I should be fine."

"I can tell you're lying Max," he replied simply.

"What?" I asked in a mix of shock and nerves. "I'm not lying."

"Yes, you are," he said again. "You just used the word 'like' half a dozen times in less than a minute. And you're fidgeting." I balled my hands into fists at my side to keep them from moving then took a deep calming breath as Matthew continued talking. "Now why don't you start again and this time, tell me the truth."

"But-" I began, only to be cut off immediately.

"I'm your stunt partner and your friend," Matthew reminded me. "Not to mention that I basically see you as a little sister. Now tell me the truth or I'll go tell TJ something's up."

"Fine." I let out a long sigh then explained things to him once again. "I was tumbling yesterday and landed weird. My ankle hurts but I don't think it's serious. Honestly. It hurts, but only every once in a while. I think I should be okay today, but I just wanted to give you the heads up on everything. That's all."

Matthew stared at me for a few minutes, as if trying to decide if I was actually telling the truth or not. I wanted to squirm under his gaze, but instead did my best to simply look him in the eyes and wait for his reply.

"If you're really hurt you should tell TJ," he suggested. "But I trust you. So for now, my lips are sealed. As long as you can perform like usual then your secret's safe with me. Are you sure it's not serious though?"

"Yeah," I said evenly, trying to keep the lie more under wraps this time.

"Okay," Matthew finally nodded, then pulled me in for a hug. "You ready to kill it?"

"Of course," I grinned.

I walked with Matthew back towards where more of our team members sat stretching and getting ready for practice. I knew it was going to be a hard one to get through, but if I could make it through the whole night without TJ and the rest of the team finding out I was injured, then it was a sign I would actually be okay. Faking it one night at practice, after all, would be good practice for faking it at Worlds. If I was still feeling any pain then.

CHAPTER 11

By some miracle, my ankle was feeling pretty good by the end of practice. It was sore overall, but I had taken ibuprofen right before leaving for the gym and it seemed to help keep the pain at a manageable level. I was able to grin and bear it most of the night, doing my best to land tumbling with the bulk of my weight on my left ankle. Matthew, of course, checked on me a few times, but since I was able to grit my teeth and power through, he seemed to back off by the end of practice. Enough so that it wasn't until I was walking to meet my dad that he brought up the injury once more.

"Message me every time you ice and elevate your ankle tomorrow," Matthew said to me quietly after practice. "I want proof you're taking care of yourself."

"Deal," I said with a serious nod.

The first message was sent to him bright and early Saturday morning as I got ready to be picked up by Tonya. I also explained to him that it was going to be a little while until I could ice and elevate it again, although I assured him that the warm water while getting a pedicure would be good for it as well. Thankfully there wasn't much swelling, and putting weight on it was only hurting a little more than it had before the long practice the night before.

Climbing into Tonya's white Jeep, I was greeted with a big hug before she drove across town to the hair salon. A year ago, we started our "girl days" as she called them, when Tonya took me to get my first real haircut. Until that point in my life, I just got my hair done with my dad when he went to the barber. But, as I learned quickly once I mentioned it at the gym, a cute short hairstyle could only be done by a hairdresser that spent all of their time working on ladies' hair. Or at least that was the impression I got when Tonya demanded I go get my hair done by her cousin. The day with her at the salon turned out to be pretty fun, so we had continued the tradition ever since. Tonya started taking me for my haircuts every few weeks after that. Adding in manicures and pedicures only happened a few times a year;

on special occasions like birthdays, getting a bid to Worlds, and, of course, before heading to Florida.

"I was thinking hair, and then maybe lunch before nails this time," Tonya listed while we drove towards The Style Shack. "I'm in dire need of barbecue and don't know how long I can wait before we go eat."

"Works for me," I agreed easily.

BBQ was the one thing, other than our love of cheer, that Tonya and I always agreed upon. She had once been a flier like me, cheering from when she was only 7 all the way through college, before opening the TNT Force gym with Nicole and TJ. The years in the gym left her with strong muscles and a thin frame, which happened to be almost as short as mine. Tonya had light brown hair, hazel eyes, and somehow always managed to look somewhat fancy. Even when she was in the gym wearing yoga pants and a bedazzled staff shirt, she looked much more mature and put together than most people her size.

Tonya was wearing a light pink cardigan over her navy dress, and of course a pair of wedge sandals that helped her look a more average height. Knowing she would dress up for our day around town like always, I tried to match her style. I was wearing a newer pair of dark jean shorts I had purchased for Florida, a red V-neck that wasn't even half as loose as my usual clothing, and the pair of gold sandals that Tonya had helped me buy a year ago on our first outing. She still looked much nicer than me with her perfectly applied makeup, but I felt like I held my own pretty well.

"So, are you getting nervous at all?" she asked, clearly referring to Worlds.

"A little," I said honestly. "I just don't want to make it all this way and mess up when it matters the most."

"I don't think you have anything to worry about," Tonya assured me. "For the first time in quite a few years I think the gym finally has a chance to bring home those first place rings."

"How's Bomb Squad been doing this week?"

It was nice to let Tonya catch me up for a while. Since none of the Worlds teams practiced on the same days or times, we didn't get to spend a lot of time in the gym together. I had a lot of friends on the Pink team that Tonya was a coach of though, so I got to hear about goings-on often enough. Gwen, who had been in my skills class during my first season at the gym, did her best to keep me in the loop about Bomb Squad. But, since our final regular season competition, everyone was a lot more focused on their own squad and the last few days of getting ready for Worlds.

"Alright, enough gym talk," Tonya announced as we pulled into a parking spot in front of The Style Shack. "Today is all about pampering ourselves. We have all next week to stress about the gym and cheer. Today I just want to focus on looking great and eating as much barbecue as possible."

I laughed, agreeing with Tonya completely as we headed into the salon and were greeted by Laura and the other workers who I had come to know over the last year. It was the start of a great day, that sadly passed much too quickly. As much as I didn't want to join Tonya for a girl's day when she invited me the first time, spending time with her was much needed. In a little way, time spent with Tonya was like having a little piece of my mom back. Thanks to losing her when I was still so young, I missed out on all the mother-daughter stuff most girls got to enjoy. So, time spent with Tonya was like making up for it little by little. Sure, nothing could ever be as good as having my mom back, but it was pretty great all the same.

"So, when were you going to tell me about your ankle?" Tonya asked as we climbed into her car after getting our nails painted. Her toes and fingers were, of course, hot pink for Bomb Squad, while mine were teal to match my Nitro uniform.

"Oh, that," I said weakly, knowing instantly that I was caught. "It's not that bad."

"Not yet," she replied. "But if you keep pushing yourself like I know you do, then it's only going to get worse."

"It was fine all last night at practice," I challenged her.

"My point exactly." Tonya gave a shake of her head, but didn't look particularly angry. "If you were on Bomb Squad you would be sitting out until you had an X-ray and an MRI, at the very least."

"I don't think it's that serious," I attempted, my voice sounding less sure than earlier. "The only times it really hurts is when I land tumbling. I let Matthew know at the start of practice yesterday so he made sure to keep a close eye on me. But it was really fine. I didn't even drop stunts or miss any of my marks in the routine at all. I mean, I don't want to tell TJ and worry him when it's nothing serious."

"I trust you," she finally said. "But I also know how stubborn you are. When we were all worried earlier this season you might have had a concussion, you were ready to get back on the mat within seconds. And that's great. It shows you have a determination and a tenacity that can't be stopped. The thing with ankle injuries though is they can go from bad to worse quickly. I know you don't want to, but taking it easy for a few days is really important. But even more importantly, you need to tell your dad."

"What?" I asked, hoping I heard her wrong. "If I tell him he'll make me go see a doctor and then I could miss Worlds altogether."

"Or you could see a doctor and they could give you tips on how to keep the injury from getting truly serious," Tonya added. "A lot of athletes compete with their ankles taped or even with braces on. There's nothing wrong with that. But you need to take those steps and do what you can so you don't get injured enough that you're out for next season. It's rare, but some injuries can keep you from ever cheering again."

I took a long breath, looking out my window at the trees and buildings passing by. We were getting closer to my house, and I knew I needed to make a decision. Telling my dad wasn't exactly what I wanted to do, but in a way, it could be better than the alternative. Tonya demanding I tell my dad was a lot better than telling my coach. Although, I realized in that moment, it might not be that simple.

"How did you know I was hurt?" I asked, turning in my seat to face Tonya once again.

"You're favoring your left foot a little bit when you walk, and you can see your ankle is swollen. I've seen enough people with injuries to notice the telltale signs of an ankle sprain like that."

"Oh," I frowned. "Do you think TJ noticed?"

"I'm not sure," she said honestly. "He has a lot to focus on when you're all in the gym. He might not have seen it yet. But he will soon if it gets worse or you keep ignoring it."

"You're not going to tell him, right?" I asked finally.

"Of course not." Tonya pulled her car over then, parking in front of my house. "As much as I'm worried for you, I would never betray your trust. We've been through a lot since you joined the gym, and even though you don't cheer on Bomb Squad with me, I still care about you just as much as any of my girls. I want to run and tell TJ that you need to go to the hospital before you can even think about touching the mat again, but I won't. I'm going to leave the decision up to you. Under one condition."

"That I tell my dad, right?" I asked.

"Right," she said with a smile. "I almost forgot about that one. So, I guess there are two conditions then. You need to tell your dad, and then if your ankle starts to get worse or in any way is keeping you from doing every part of Nitro's routine, then you tell TJ. Immediately. No questions asked."

I thought about her demands for a minute, realizing all that it meant. If my ankle got better, it wouldn't matter one way or the other. Or, if the injury was more serious and it got worse, then it could mean missing performing at Worlds. And as much as I believed in my team, I knew my tumbling and flying added a lot of points to our score sheet. Not being on the mat would mean almost no chance of Nitro making it to finals. But, I realized finally, there would always be next year. Or the year after that. Chances to win would be around every year, so keeping my ankle ready for future seasons was kind of a big deal in the long run.

"Deal," I finally decided with a sigh. "If it gets any worse, I'll tell TJ right away. I promise."

CHAPTER 12

"Is this going to take long?" I asked my dad, pausing my furious typing on my phone. I was sending a message to Matthew, letting him know I was sitting in an exam room waiting for Dr. Hapkin. Matthew was the only person I could really talk to about everything, since I knew telling Connor would likely mean TJ finding out immediately.

"I don't know," he replied honestly. "We can get ice cream after this if it makes you feel any better."

"It doesn't make me feel much better," I answered with a frown. "But it might help a little."

My dad just let out a laugh then went back to reading the National Geographic magazine he had been looking through after finding it in the waiting room. When I got home from my day out with Tonya, my dad had been out in the backyard mowing the lawn. I hardly had time to tell him I was hurt before he loaded me in the car and rushed me to the walk-in clinic. His khaki shorts and white shirt still smelled like fresh cut grass and his hair was still damp with sweat. As with most weekends, he traded his contacts for his glasses, their thick frames making his worried expressions on the ride even more dramatic.

"I'm fine you know," I said again, although I knew it did little to change my current situation.

"We'll see what Eliot says about that."

That was one of the bad things about having a dad that knew every doctor in town. Simply taking me to the clinic wasn't good enough. He called ahead, made sure the best doctor was on hand waiting and told them to "warm up the MRI machine" before we left the house. I knew it all meant he cared, but it felt like overkill considering my ankle didn't hurt all that much anymore. There was nothing I could do about it though, especially once Dr. Hapkin entered the room.

"Brian, good to see you." he grinned. He gave my dad a firm handshake before turning to me with a serious look on his face. "Max, I hear you had an accident."

"It's nothing major," I quickly assured him. "I just landed wrong when I was doing a kick double full and my ankle hurts a little."

Thankfully, Dr. Hapkin knew I was an all-star cheerleader, so I didn't have to explain myself over and over again. Sure, he didn't quite know what a kick double full was, but he could guess what it might entail. He had seen a few videos of my routines since I joined the TNT Force gym, so unlike a lot of people, he understood just how serious an injury could be when it happened on the all-star cheer mat versus a sideline cheerleader that wasn't thrown in the air as often as I was.

"Alright, let's take a look," he said to me, moving closer to examine my ankle.

Dr. Hapkin began by testing to see what area of my ankle was causing me pain. He worked methodically, hardly applying pressure while still assessing the injury. Moments like that were always a little shocking considering he was a larger man, made up of equal parts muscle and general bulk. Between his size, his thick beard, and shaved head, he could be rather intimidating at first. Or at least to those that didn't have him over often for barbecues and days spent around the pool. After seeing him compete with my dad in a rather intense cannonball competition the first summer we lived in Texas, he was a lot less intense than the first time I met him at a work party for my dad's office.

"Ouch!" I yelped, not expecting the slight turn of my ankle to cause the instant shooting pain I was feeling.

"So, no more of that then," Dr. Hapkin said with a smile, moving my foot back to sit in a way that wouldn't damage it further. "Let's get you in for an x-ray and see what's really going on in there."

By "an x-ray," he really meant an x-ray, an MRI, and then a long conversation with my dad that I found hard to understand. They went back and forth while looking over my test results, pointing at a tiny mark on both transparent images they had hanging on the backlit portion of the wall. Through their debating, I heard a few words I was hoping were just speculation. Words like sprain, tear, and break were never good when it came to sports injuries. But when they finally decided to welcome me into the conversation I was happy to hear it was rather minor as far as ankle injuries were concerned.

"So, I just need to wrap it and be careful?" I asked after listening to both of them explain everything to me.

"Being careful might not be enough," my dad said simply.

"If you push yourself too much the injury can become serious pretty fast," Dr. Hapkin added. "All-star cheerleading is high impact, and your ankle is right on the brink of some severe consequences from all the tumbling and jumping. You should stay off it for a week or two so you can make sure it doesn't get worse before it can get better."

"I can't miss Worlds!"

"We know." My dad said the words while holding up his hands in mock surrender. It was a little odd, but considering my distressed tone, it also seemed appropriate. "He said you 'should,' not that you need to. Instead, we're going to get you some tape and a brace and I can talk to TJ when-"

"No," I quickly cut him off. "We can't tell TJ."

My dad paused before asking the obvious, "And why is that?"

"If he knows, he won't let me cheer," I frowned. "But I have to cheer. I have to compete at Worlds and be there for Nitro."

"I'll let you two chat this one out." Dr. Hapkin could clearly tell our conversation wasn't going to be an easy one for either of us. So, after shaking my dad's hand and him wishing me good luck, he left the exam room. Knowing that talking in the car was a better idea than in the doctor's office, I followed my dad outside before we continued where we left off.

"Don't you think TJ is going to notice you're wearing a brace at practice?"

"Maybe," I said with a shrug. "But we only have two more practices until I leave for

85

Florida. I can get a lot of rest until then. Promise."

"That might not be enough sweetie," my dad explained with the shake of his head. "Rest won't mean much once you start running full outs and have to take the Worlds stage."

"But I have a few more days until I need to worry about that, right?"

Starting the car, my dad thought about everything for another second, leaving me to wait in silence. I wasn't sure what he was thinking or what he was going to say, but it felt like everything hung in the balance. If my dad said I had to tell TJ, then it was going to make the week even more stressful than it was already sure to be. After all, going up against the best teams in the world wasn't going to exactly be easy, even after such a great season.

"When we get home, we're calling TJ," he began finally.

"We can't," I said again. "I promised Tonya I would tell him if things got worse, but I can't tell him now. I'll be stuck on the sidelines for sure if he knew."

"Okay then," my dad began again. I could tell he wanted to honor my deal with Tonya but also still look out for me. "Then I'm making a call to Emma's mom so she can keep an eye on you until I get to Florida."

He continued, telling me I needed to ice and elevate my leg every chance I had before I left, and then also to call him after every practice in Florida to let him know how I was feeling. I listened, a smile growing on my face. I knew once I rested more I would be fine. In fact, I was certain that when my dad arrived at Worlds Friday evening after wrapping up his week of clinical trials, he would see that I wasn't just fine, but better than ever. My ankle wasn't going to get in the way of winning Worlds, or even in the way of the fun week with my friends before we competed.

"Now when we get home you're going to ice it and elevate it while I go get a few brace options to try out." He spoke while slowly driving out of the parking lot.

"We're still getting ice cream, right?" I asked immediately.

"Yes," he laughed. "We're still getting ice cream. If we skipped out I know I'd never hear the end of it."

"So true," I agreed, then pulled out my phone to update Matthew again.

CHAPTER 13

Despite wanting to get my packing done on Sunday, I spent most of the day resting. I kept ice on my ankle and kept it elevated. Thankfully, it did the trick. Despite the long and grueling practice on Monday evening, my ankle was holding up okay. I made sure to keep it wrapped, covered by my knee-high yellow socks. They were part of a Minions outfit Emma and I both wore for the Disney dress up day. I suggested we add the socks to the costume last minute to "look cute." The real reason was that it allowed me to have some extra support for my stunts and tumbling. TJ, or anyone else for that matter, couldn't see the brace as easily through the thick socks. By the time I finally walked into the gym Tuesday, I was more focused on the final Nitro practice than I was on my ankle. The swelling was completely gone, and the pain was barely noticeable.

"You should have told me you were wearing socks again tonight!" Emma gushed, running towards me as I slipped my backpack into one of the open cubbies next to the mat. I noticed she was holding the face paint and black lipstick in her hands. "Ready for makeup?"

"Thanks," I said in reply to her compliment on my socks. "I think I'm just going to do a line of paint under each of my eyes. You know, like what football players always have."

"Great idea," she nodded, handing me the makeup. "There's more if you need it. Jade has some in the bathroom."

"This should be good," I shrugged, then walked to the mirror against the wall to apply the paint. It took only seconds, giving me time to return the paint and remove my hoodie before taking a seat on the mat to stretch. My ankle was feeling good, but stretching it to get ready for the coming routine was super important.

"You don't have your phone out?" Connor asked, sitting down next to me. He was wearing a camo shirt and had drawn three lines across his face in a diagonal pattern that stretched from his right temple down to the left side of his jaw.

"My phone?" I asked, then immediately remembered that much like our Disney dress up practice, there were sure to be selfies and photos galore for the camo night. "Oh, I left it in my bag,"

"I got it," he laughed. He quickly stood up, jogged to my bag, and then returned to where I was sitting to hand me my phone. "Can I have the first selfie of the night as a reward?"

"I guess," I said, adding in an eye roll for effect. Connor simply laughed, then leaned in for the photo.

We took a few more photos, changing our facial expressions in each one. Then, as expected, I took more and more photos with other members of Nitro. In most shots, we gave 'tough' faces or would try to flex our muscles. The idea was to make everyone else getting ready for Worlds see just how prepared we were to put up a good fight. I knew if no one stopped us, the photos would go on forever. But, thankfully, TJ called everyone to the center of the mat before we took up the whole evening with selfies.

"Before we get started, we have something we need to do," TJ explained. He was sitting facing all of us, his camo cargo shorts and black shirt matching our practice wear. "I need everyone to take off their bows."

His words were not what we expected, but the girls on the team began removing their bows all the same. A few people needed help removing bobby pins or untangling hair ties, but before long none of the 16 girls on Nitro had a bow in their hair.

"Take a look at your bows please," he continued. "Boys, you can look at a bow near you. Now, tell me what you see."

There was a pause, as everyone tried to figure out what was really going on. The bows we were all holding had been our team practice bows since we won our Worlds bid in December. It was a tick tock bow, featuring two different patterns of ribbon for the base. One side was covered in a mix of flags from around the world, making up the top left loop and bottom right tale of the large bow. The other half of the bow was a white ribbon with 2017 on the tail in glittery blue lettering, and a world with the word 'BID' over it on the loop. They were a small way to show everyone we had earned a chance to perform at Worlds and helped us to focus on Worlds at practice all season.

"They're our bid bows," someone finally said, causing a lot more people to nod.

"Yeah," Matthew agreed. "They show everyone we belong at Worlds."

"And they show the other countries that might be there," another athlete said.

"Okay," TJ nodded. "You're all correct. These bows show the people watching that you made it to Worlds, but like you said other people will be there. In fact, with very few exceptions, everyone there could also wear these bows thanks to winning their own bids during the season. Which is why I'm taking back all of your bows."

Reaching into his cargo pockets, TJ pulled out a trash bag and held it open. I sat staring at him in shock, certain I was misunderstanding what he was telling us to do. But then, I watched as Emma stood up and moved to put her bow in the bag. Then Addison did the same, followed by Sammy and Kenna. Knowing I needed to do the same, I got up carefully and placed my bow in the quickly filling bag. As I returned to my seat between Connor and Jade, I was at least relieved to see everyone looked as confused as I felt. The confusion that grew as TJ got up and walked the bag into the office. We sat in stunned silence until he returned with a large black gift bag.

"You'll get your bows back, but not just yet," he explained. "After today we can't think about things we earned or deserved. Once we get to Florida everything starts fresh. We only win if we earn it on the Worlds stage. So tonight, you get a new bow."

Turning the bag upside down TJ poured a pile of black, green, and tan fabric onto the blue mat. Once everything settled I saw it was actually a bunch of camo bows and bandanas. Unlike after TJ took us he needed our bid bows, no one seemed to pause even a second. Instead, everyone moved into action, grabbing a bow while celebrating the new items. Much like my phone, Connor grabbed a bow for me when he moved to grab his bandana. I thanked him, then went to work putting the bow in my hair.

"I'll give you two minutes for photos or anything else you need to do," TJ called out over the celebration and general noise on the mat. Everyone quieted down when he spoke though, so I could clearly hear the words we all knew were coming. "Then we start conditioning."

CHAPTER 14

"I finally won," Matthew called out to me when I entered the gym after finishing my warm-up run.

As always, we completed three miles of running to start practice. Everyone was much better at running the full distance than when the season began at the start of summer, but three miles was still long enough to leave people tired by the end. And this time, I was feeling the run like never before. In fact, it was the first time all season I didn't finish first; instead coming in fourth.

"Guess so," I said simply. I knew I could have pushed myself so I came in first, but also knew that taking it easy was a better idea for my ankle.

"Even the best fall sometimes I guess," he grinned.

"Fall, or take it easy so she can crush everyone during practice?" Connor said in reply, coming to my aid.

Matthew had no response, instead taking a long drink from his water bottle before sitting down on the blue mat to stretch. I did the same, sitting a few feet away from him. It wasn't until I was sitting down that I remembered that I didn't grab my water as I planned. With a sigh, I started standing up to walk to my bag when Connor took a seat next to me, handing me my water while taking a drink of his. I took the teal container from him and enjoyed a long sip before turning to him.

"Thanks," I said with a smile.

"Let me know if you need anything else," he said quietly, as if to keep Matthew or anyone else from hearing.

"Wait," I said suddenly, replaying the numerous times he had helped me since I got to the gym. Not only had he grabbed my phone and water, he also made sure to encourage me during the final lap around the gym during our run, even slowing down so he finished directly after me despite being able to go much faster. "Why are you being so nice today?"

"Matthew told me." When I didn't immediately reply, he continued. "But even if he hadn't, I still knew something was up. I saw your live video the other day. Laughing it off may have fooled Lexi and Halley, but I saw the look on your face when you landed that kick double. It was the same face you made during your fall at the start of the season."

The fall he was talking about was not a moment I liked to think about often. It was just a few weeks into the season as I was working with a new stunt group to figure out who I would be paired with all season. During a rather basic stunt, one of my then teammates made a mistake that sent me tumbling to the ground. There was nothing I could do to stop the fall, but thankfully Juleah jumped under me to keep me from slamming my head into the mat. It saved me from a much more serious injury, but still knocked the wind out of me and left Juleah with a bloody nose and black eye. I had watched a video of it only once and immediately tried my best to block it from my mind. But for someone who saw it happen in person, it was clearly little harder to forget.

"Connor please-" I began, only to be cut off.

"I won't say anything," he assured me. "As long as you stay safe. A little tweak is fine, but if it's anything serious you need to do something before it gets worse and you can't even compete in Florida."

"Deal," I said with a sigh. "If I can just get through tonight then I'll be good to go. I can rest it all day tomorrow and push through at Worlds easily."

Connor nodded, but I could tell he was still feeling a bit unsure about it. Although I had only known him for a little over a year and a half, Connor was as much a brother to me as Peter and Kyle. He was one of my first friends at the gym, and after a whole season on Nitro together, we were closer than ever. I knew I could trust him to keep my secret, but, like he hinted, he was also going to do what was best for me. That meant that if things got worse he would make sure I got help, even if I wasn't quite ready to ask for it.

I reminded myself of that as we continued our conditioning and began to warm up our tumbling. I did my best to land with more of my weight on my left foot every time like I had the night before. And it was working. Everything was feeling great. So much so that when we got to our first partner stunt I was barely even thinking about my ankle. Instead, I ignored everything but the skill I was about to perform and the timing in which I needed to perform it.

"1-3-5-7," TJ counted out, leading everyone into the first stunt of the routine.

Matthew was standing behind me, his hands holding firm on my waist. I held his wrists, pushing off with my arms as well as my legs after bending my knees low to the ground for an added boost. As I was tossed up into the air thanks to the push of my legs and also Matthew's toss, I spun around once before being caught by my left foot. I held my right foot next to my head, holding it in place in a move called a heel stretch. Then, as TJ continued to count out the beats I traded my legs so I was holding my left leg up by my head while Matthew had a firm grip on my right foot.

As Matthews's hands grabbed my foot to hold it in place, I could feel the pressure building in my ankle. Then, as Matthew removed one of his hands from his grip on my shoe I could feel the pain intensify. It was instantly clear something was wrong. The realization caused me to wobble just enough that Matthew needed to bring me back down out of the air two counts early. Although a small thing for some people, it would be a deduction at Worlds. A fact that had TJ calling out to me right away.

"Max, don't get lazy on me," he announced while clapping the beat for the other stunt teams. "You can do this in your sleep. Don't lose your focus now. Let's try it again everyone. Don't think I missed your fall either Stephanie."

I breathed a sigh of relief that TJ's reaction was rather standard. He rarely had to talk to me about mistakes, since I could go through a week of practice without missing a tumbling pass or a flying skill. So when he didn't draw more attention to my error, I had a feeling it meant he hadn't picked up on my injury as quickly as Tonya. That fact had me genuinely happy. Or at least it did until I turned and saw the look on Matthew's face.

"Are you okay?" I asked him, although I pretty much knew the reply that was sure to follow.

"I'm fine," he said simply. "Let's talk about you, Max."

"I'm good," I shrugged.

"Max," he tried again, his tone much more serious. "I know you. I've spent more time holding you in the air than I care to calculate, so I know you better than just about anyone on this mat." His eyes quickly flicked towards the far corner of the mat where TJ was talking to Connor and Mary. "When you eat a big lunch, I can tell. Did you really think I wouldn't notice what just happened?"

"What's going on?" Liz finally asked. She had been standing listening to us without really understanding. But, as our spotter for the partner stunt, letting her know about everything was just as important as telling Matthew on Friday evening.

"She's hurt," Matthew said quietly after looking around to make sure no one else was listening in. "It's minor for now, but you need to make sure you brace her right ankle if she starts to wobble at all. Got it?"

"Got it." Liz turned to me, a serious look on her face. "If you need help wrapping it later let me know. I sprained my ankle a few years ago and got really good at taping it so I could still tumble."

I looked at Liz in shock for a second, then thanked her. Despite knowing her for only a few months she seemed to immediately understand why I didn't want everyone to know about my injury. Since the start of the season, I got to know Liz well thanks to being paired with her for partner stunts. Much like Juleah, she was tall and muscular, two qualities that were great for a back spot. Liz had poker straight black hair that only made her dark complexion look even more flawless. When she wasn't on the mat, Liz was always reading and generally kept to herself. But, on the cheer floor, she was the perfect person to have under me in case I took a tumble out of the air.

"One more time," TJ called out, finally pulling me away from my moment with Liz and Matthew. "5-6-7-8."

This time, as I made the switch from my left leg to my right I could again feel the searing pain, but was able to keep my body position. This was thanks to Liz following the advice Matthew had given her. It allowed me to stand on my ankle without wobbling around. It allowed me to ignore the pain once Matthew was the only one holding me, and with one hand no less, so I didn't come out of the air early. The only problem was that even with the added support, it was clear the first attempt had an effect on my ankle. Despite the basic movement of the tick-tock heel stretch, it was like my ankle could no longer keep up with the physical demands of flying. But, I knew I needed to put on a brave face. Not only was my dad watching from the parent viewing area, TJ was watching. And if I couldn't convince him I was doing okay, then I would have to explain the full extent of my injury to him. Something I knew had the potential of hurting worse than any ankle pain.

CHAPTER 15

Making it through practice was harder than ever, but in the end, I survived. Matthew was worried about me all evening, and I noticed Connor also watching me from across the cheer mat. It made pretending to be okay harder, but I did my best to push through. Sure, my ankle was in more and more pain as the night went on, but no one needed to know. Instead, I put on a brave face during practice, then did the same once I got home. I only prayed my dad would believe my performance, as well as Peter who came by after practice to help me get ready for my early morning flight.

"I feel like this is way harder than it should be," Peter said to me as he carried another shirt out of my closet.

"Nope, not that one," I said again with a frown. "I should just get it myself."

"You try and I'll go tattle on you," he replied immediately. "You know your dad said to rest."

"Fine," I sighed. "Now try again. It's a black shirt with white letters and silver rhinestones."

We continued like this for a while. I would describe the items I wanted him to find, and Peter would fail a few times before finally landing on the one I was looking for. All of this was done while I sat on my bed, my ankle propped up atop a mountain of pillows. As silly as it was, it was another way to get my dad to worry a little less about my injury. Not to mention it allowed me to get more done than I would on my own. Best of all though, was that the elevation and ice pack proved to be a much-needed relief after practice.

"This has to be it," Peter said, emerging from my closet once again.

"Finally," I replied with a smile. "Okay, now you need to find my dark jean shorts, and my three nicest pairs of basketball shorts."

"How about a break?" he asked. He quickly folded my shirt and placed it in the open suitcase on the floor then moved to sit down next to me on my bed. "If you can't even pack your own suitcase today how are you going to keep TJ from seeing that you're injured tomorrow?"

"I'm going to wear jeans to the airport," I began slowly. "Then once we get to Florida I'll think of something."

"What if it doesn't work?"

"It has to," I insisted. "I have to be on that Worlds stage. But if TJ finds out I'm injured then all of that could go away."

"Would he really make you sit out for something so small though?"

"Maybe," I shrugged. "I'm not sure. We haven't had any big injuries this year, so I don't know what he would do. But if there's even a slight chance I won't get to perform, then I have to keep it a secret."

"Okay," he nodded. "What happens if you perform at Worlds and get hurt even worse?"

"Then I'll get better," I said simply. "I know it might be hard for you to understand but this is the most important thing ever. After Summit last year, all I've wanted to do is make it to Worlds and help the gym finally prove we deserve to win. The look on Connor's, Matthew's, and Emma's face after they lost last year has been my motivation all season. I know there's a lot of people who have wanted to perform at Worlds for way longer than me, but I still want it just as bad as them. And nothing is going to get in the way of finally reaching that goal."

"I get it," Peter replied. "You know, you've always done sports, but I've never seen you love something and put your whole heart into it the way you do with cheer. It's clear to everyone how much you love it. I just don't want you to get hurt over some jacket when you don't need to."

"Rings," I corrected him instantly. "You win jackets at NCA, rings at Summit and Worlds."

Peter nodded and I knew he was making a mental note so he wouldn't mess it up again. Or, possibly, he made the note to not mention anything about NCA if at all possible. After all, it was the one sore spot in an otherwise amazing season. Nitro easily grabbed first place at all but two competitions that year. Once, at our first comp after the Christmas break, we got third. Then, with everyone watching at nationals we had some major mistakes in our pyramid on day two and we ended up in fifth. It was especially hard for everyone who had been on the team last season for Worlds since it was a pyramid fail that had once again kept them from winning first.

"Just promise me you'll be careful, okay?" Peter's words pulled me out of my memories about NCA. I turned to look at him and was surprised to see a very serious look on his face. "No one's going to be happy if you go out there on day one and push yourself so hard you end up missing out on finals completely."

"I'll try," I agreed. "I just can't let my team down. We need this win."

"And you'll get it," he said simply. "Those other teams don't stand a chance against you."

"You're only saying that because-"

"I'm saying that because it's true," Peter interrupted. He leaned closer to me before speaking again. "Even injured you're one of the best cheerleaders out there. When you get on that stage it's impossible to remember you're not a girly girl all the time. Not to sound cliché, but you really shine and sparkle out there. It makes it impossible for people to look at anyone but you for the whole routine. Or at least it makes it impossible for me to look at anyone else."

As much as I wanted to tell Peter he was only trying to be nice or was just making things up, I knew he was serious. The look on his face was much more intense than usual. It was a look I had seen only one other time; the week I first got my hair cut short for cheer. Even after seeing the now familiar facial expression then, it was no easier to take in this time around.

"Thanks Peter," I said earnestly.

I expected Peter to stand up and go back to helping me pack, or at the very least lean away from me. But instead, he just sat there and continued to look at me. Something about it was a little strange and made me feel like I was supposed to say something. Before I got the chance, however, Peter stood up and bolted off my bed to the open suitcase on the floor. I opened my mouth to ask him what was going on when my dad walked into the room.

"How's packing coming?" he asked, leaning on the door frame.

"Slow," Peter replied, the look from just moments ago gone from his face. "Max has too many clothes."

"Never thought I would hear that one and believe it," my dad laughed. He paused then spoke to me, "You okay Max?"

"Yeah," I managed, although I was beyond confused. "What are we doing for dinner?"

"I was just about to ask you the same thing."

As my dad and I began going over some food options, I kept an eye on Peter. He was still acting a little odd, looking at me when he thought I wasn't paying attention. The strange expression was a thing of the past, but something was still different. I hoped I could get to the bottom of it, but once my dad decided to start making dinner, Peter said a quick goodbye and made a beeline for the door."

"You aren't going to even say goodbye?" I asked Peter as he focused on his phone while following my dad out of my room.

"Oh yeah," he mumbled. He walked over to stand next to me, then shocked me a bit when he leaned down and gave me a hug. "Have a good trip."

"Uh, thanks," I managed, still in shock from his embrace.

Then, just like that, Peter was gone. He walked out of my room then out of the house. It all happened in a few seconds, leaving me unsure what to do next. I looked at the half empty suitcase and my open closet door and knew I needed to get ready for Florida one way or the other. Swinging my legs over to touch the ground I stood up gradually, putting as little pressure on my right ankle as possible. Then, nice and slowly, I moved to my closet to get back to work.

CHAPTER 16

"What are you doing here?" I asked in shock Wednesday morning as I climbed out of my dad's car.

"We couldn't let you leave without saying goodbye!" Lexi exclaimed, then moved to wrap me up in a massive hug.

Lexi's hug was followed by one from Halley who was also standing on the sidewalk as we drove up to the airport. After a long night finishing up all my packing once Peter left, I barely slept thanks to the building excitement. Knowing I was going to be heading to Worlds in the morning made falling asleep next to impossible. But, after a few fitful hours attempting to not be awake, I got up and helped load the car. The sun was still only just beginning to rise when we began the drive across town, so when I saw my best friends waiting for me in the headlights of the car, I was shocked, to say the least.

"Aren't you going to miss school?" I asked, although I was glad they were there.

"We might be a little late," Halley admitted. "But we couldn't miss this!"

While my dad began unloading my bags from the trunk, my friends went on and on about how excited they were for me, how proud they were of me, and wished me good luck about a million times. They walked with me as we headed to the security area where Emma and her parents were waiting for me. It was where I was going to have to say goodbye to both of my friends, not to mention where I had to say goodbye to my dad.

"Text us every day," Halley reminded me as we stood near the security entrance.

"No," Lexi corrected. "Every hour. And send lots of Snapchats so we know what you're up to."

"You're going to do so great!" Halley finally exclaimed, then closed the gap between us to give me yet another hug.

Lexi joined the hug, an embrace that lasted much longer than expected. Clearly the idea of not seeing me for a week was something none of us was looking forward to. Other than an end of summer vacation my dad and I had taken to New York to see my aunt, I never went more than a day or two without seeing my best friends. But now I was leaving them behind as I attended the first competition of my cheerleading career that they wouldn't be present for. At other competitions, they were on the sidelines cheering for me while I performed. This would be the first time they were miles away, left to cheer for me on from the other side of a phone or computer screen.

"Well we should go," Lexi said rather reluctantly. The comment was made after my dad cleared his throat, likely as a hint that I needed to get moving. "Have a good trip."

Giving my friends one final hug, I couldn't help but frown as I watched them walk back towards the exit. I gave a quick wave to Halley's mom who was waiting for them. Lexi's mom was likely at home getting Matthew ready to leave for the airport as well. His flight was leaving a little later, allowing him to take a test in the morning before heading to Florida.

"Here's your bag slip and ticket," my dad explained, handing me the two rectangles of paper. He had used the time I spent with my friends to check in my bag and get a paper copy of my tickets printed. "You have everything else, right?"

"Yup," I nodded. "My uniform, bows, and shoes are in my carry on, and I have the extra cash in my bag in case anything happens."

My dad nodded for a second, then

pulled me in for a hug. He wrapped his arms around me tighter than usual, clearly not quite ready to say goodbye to me just yet.

"You know you're going to see me in two days, right?" I asked with a laugh.

"I know," he replied, finally letting go. "I just wish I could be there for every second. This is your first time at Worlds after all."

"You'll be there for the important stuff," I assured him. "Like when we win the final round on Monday."

That seemed to satisfy my dad enough for the time being, mostly since he had gone through the checklist with me twice before we even left the house. As much as I wanted to be annoyed by it, I knew it was just his way of making sure I was okay until he arrived later in the week. Thankfully, instead of continuing to grill me, he pulled me in for yet another hug before planting a kiss on my forehead and then sending me off to finally join Emma.

"You ready?" she asked simply.

"More than anything in the whole world," I replied. Then, noticing my unintended pun, I joined Emma in a quick giggle.

We made it through security quickly, then made our way to gate 4 where we saw a few fellow TNT Force gym members waiting for us. It was easy to spot everyone since we were all wearing our pink, lime green, or teal 'Ready For Worlds' shirts, although some were covered with black TNT hoodies. Much like my trip to Summit the year before, the gym gave us very specific instruction on what we could and could not wear during our time at Worlds. It included a lot of special clothing, bows, and even new uniform bags from Dehen, the same company that made our uniforms. But I put those thoughts out of my mind as Connor came walking up to me with a grin on his face.

"Good morning," he smiled, handing me a cupcake decorated with bright teal icing. "You don't need to eat it now, but my mom made them for the whole team."

"It's perfect," I assured him, giving him a quick hug while making sure to keep my cupcake safe. "I'm totally eating this now though. Cupcakes for breakfast are great energy for traveling."

"Sounds about right to me," he laughed. "How's your ankle."

His question was little more than a whisper, despite the fact that Emma and anyone else from the gym was at least a few steps away. I appreciated it though, since I was still determined to not let TJ know the news.

"Feels good," I shrugged while peeling off my cupcake wrapper. "Today will be a good chance to rest it more too. I should be fine for tomorrow."

While Connor told me he was happy to hear the news and then began explaining how he was planning to trade seats with the person sitting next to me, I tried to keep a straight face. The truth was, even standing next to Connor in the airport was more painful than I wanted to admit. I wasn't sure what it was that had happened during the stunt the night before, but it was a growing problem. Literally. My ankle was swollen despite the ice and elevation the night before. The worst part was that I knew I should tell TJ. I promised my dad, Tonya, and Matthew that I would let my coach know if the injury became more serious. But, as I glanced towards my coach as Connor spoke, I knew I wasn't going to give him the news. The mere thought of not getting to perform on the final stage at Worlds was too big of a risk, even with the seriousness of my injury.

CHAPTER 17

"What's up with your ankle?"

The second the words were out of Emma's month on Wednesday night, I knew I was in trouble. We had arrived at our hotel room after stopping on the way from the airport for dinner. With the sun just beginning to set, we all raced to our rooms and started getting ready for some time in the pool. I was thankful to be rooming with Emma, Juleah, and Addison, since they were some of my best friends on Nitro. The only problem, I learned in that moment, was that it was going to be hard to keep my injury from my friends all week when we were staying in the same small room together.

"Oh, that," I said, trying to buy myself some time. But, I knew immediately that I needed to tell the truth. "I kind of got hurt a few days ago. It's okay though."

"Are you sure?" Emma asked again. "It looks really bad."

I glanced down and had to admit she was right. It was still just as swollen as it had been the day before, despite the long time resting it on the flights. Connor even managed to get a seat next to me and let me rest my feet on his lap for the longer of our two flights to help elevate it even more. It clearly wasn't enough, and knowing that I was about to be around the whole team while at the pool, I needed to think of something fast.

"My dad took me to the doctor and they're not really worried," I spoke quickly. "It looks a lot worse than it is, especially after the long day of travel. It just gets a little swollen by the end of the day when I'm walking around a lot. But it hasn't been hurting me at all during practice. Even when I was doing my hardest tumbling."

Emma seemed to be convinced, although she gave my leg another long look before turning to dig in her suitcase for her flip flops. I turned around, thankful that she was buying the explanation for the time being. I adjusted the straps of my bright blue bathing suit top, all the while trying to think of a way to somehow cover my ankle while I was swimming. If TJ spotted it as easily as Emma did, then I was in trouble for sure. And wearing the brace my dad had chosen for me on Friday clearly wasn't an option.

"You should spend time in the hot tub," Emma said, as if reading my mind. "Then people won't see it and the water will be really good for it."

"Thanks," I replied simply.

"I know it's more serious than you're letting on Max," she added quietly, stepping closer to me. Juleah and Addison were listening to music in the bathroom while fixing their hair and makeup, so I knew they couldn't hear us even when we were talking at a normal volume. "But I know how stubborn you are. If you need help wrapping it or anything let me know. Or if you need me to cover for you at all. But I really want you to be careful. An ankle injury can go from bad to super bad in no time at all if you're not careful. Taking a day off from practice to really make sure you're good to perform when it counts might be a good idea."

"I'll keep that in mind," I nodded.

Before Emma could say anything else, I opened the door and thankfully saw Connor and Matthew standing there about to knock. Despite the fact that both of them also knew of my injury, I used it as a chance to change the subject and head down to the pool. Leaving our roommates behind, Emma and I walked with the guys, chatting easily about other cheer teams as we went.

The best thing about Worlds was that I was getting to see some of the teams I hadn't seen since NCA. Sure, I could watch routines online anytime I wanted, but getting to see everyone in person was always exciting for me. Not because I looked up to certain teams or cheerleaders the way I knew other people did, but because watching them made me want to push myself even harder.

"I should do that," Emma announced after Matthew mentioned running into a popular cheer vlogger on his way to our room. "Vlogging can't be that hard, right?"

"I guess not," I agreed, laughing at the determined look on her face.

"The editing might be hard," Connor chimed in. "Especially if you film a whole lot."

"Well, I can deal with that later," Emma decided aloud. Then, she pulled out her phone, turned the camera on and got started. "Hey YouTube, I'm Emma and this is Matthew, Connor, and Max. Welcome to my Worlds vlog!"

Emma continued to talk to the camera as we walked through the Worlds Village and to the pool. We arrived to see a few other people around, but since it was just the start of the week at Worlds, the pool was not as crowded as we worried it might have been. Instead, we easily found some deck chairs for our stuff then all headed into the hot tub at Emma's suggestion. She, of course, continued to vlog while we were in the water, assuring all of us that her phone and case were waterproof so there was no need to worry about damage if she dropped her phone.

"Okay, time for a serious interview," Emma announced into the camera, leaning in closer to me as she spoke. "Max, this is your first time at Worlds. What are you most excited for?"

"Winning," I said simply.

There was a pause after I spoke, then my friends all laughed. Matthew made a comment about the fact that he loved how confident I was, but at the same time didn't try to correct me. It was as if everyone was on the same page, agreeing that it was finally going to be Nitro's year to make it to finals and take home the gold once and for all.

"Oh good, TJ's here," Emma all but yelled just seconds after Matthew's comment. She quickly raced out of the hot tub, shouting questions at our coach even before she reached him on the pool deck.

"We're going to have to listen to her vlog all weekend now," I said with a sigh.

"Not us," Matthew reminded me. "We're not rooming with her. You're the one that's going to hear it from sun up to sundown."

Splashing a little water at Matthew in my frustration I leaned back in the hot tub and tried to relax. Without Emma there to ask questions and go on and on with her brand-new vlog, it was much more peaceful. Even with more and more members of Nitro arriving at the pool for the evening, the hot tub was like a little oasis. Or at least it was until Matthew turned to me with a question I should have seen coming.

"How's the ankle?" His question was simple enough, especially since he wasn't there at the airport when everyone else left. But it still gave me instant anxiety.

"Good," I answered slowly. "I iced it all last night after practice, so that helped a lot."

"She elevated it on the plane too," Connor added, thankfully coming to my rescue.

"Yeah, I saw the Snapchats." Matthew's comment was accompanied with a raised eyebrow, but he continued before I could overthink it too much. "Are you sure you're going to be able to go full out on your stunts and tumbling tomorrow?"

"Yeah," I said with as much confidence as I could manage. "I'm not worried about it at all."

"Just because you're not worried doesn't mean everything's fine," Matthew replied. To my horror, Connor nodded in agreement. "You need to wear a brace tomorrow even if it means TJ sees it."

I said a simple, "Okay," then got quiet as Gwen made a rather splashy entrance into the hot tub. As a member of Bomb Squad, I didn't see her a lot at the gym, but she had been in my stunt class the months leading into me getting placed onto Nitro, so she was a good friend still. Gwen had hair that was a similar shade of brown as mine, although her hair extended almost to her waist. She was also a lot taller than me, and had a frame that was filled out with lots of muscles while still allowing her to look super cute in her white and red bikini. In fact, her strength was one of the reasons she was the center base on Bomb Squad. Lifting a person up by yourself wasn't exactly easy, but Gwen managed it every time she stepped foot on the mat to perform.

"So, are you ready for this week?" she asked me, oblivious to the conversation that had just been going on in the warm water.

"Of course," I answered, while Matthew and Connor gave similar replies as well. "What about you? Do you think Bomb Squad is going to finally bring home first?"

"Fingers crossed," she said with a frown. "We can't seem to hit our pyramid consistently anymore, so it will be a miracle if we make it to finals."

As the conversation turned to stunts, pyramids, and other cheerleading talk, I breathed a sigh of relief. The less everyone focused on my ankle, the better. In the back of my mind though, I tried to remember what Matthew had said. Wearing my ankle brace for team practice in the morning was going to be key. The only problem was finding a way to pull off my plan. Without the aid of costumes like at the last two team practices, I knew I was going to have to get pretty creative so everything could go how I wanted it to.

CHAPTER 18

"Say good morning to the vlog," Emma's voice all but yelled into my ear the following morning.

I groaned and rolled over, trying to avoid the camera I knew was in my face. It was silent for only a few seconds, then the noise level was back as Emma began attempting to wake up Juleah and Addison as well. She was clearly still on her YouTube kick, something I hoped would fade the longer we spent in Florida. Ignoring her, I got out of bed and began putting into action the plan I came up with the night before.

After staying at the pool until TJ encouraged all of us to get back to our rooms to get some sleep, I returned to my room more than happy to head to bed. Or at least that was the plan until I remembered I needed to come up with something so my injury would go unnoticed. Thankfully, the inspiration was waiting for me when we got back to our room and saw the goody bags that were waiting for us on the beds.

Much like when I arrived at Summit there was a large pile of gifts for each team member. The new team items included a white 'Worlds 2017' shirt with the TNT Force logo on the sleeve, a grey tank top with 'NITRO' in rhinestones on the front, and a lot of Disney items. We were given Mickey ears with the TNT Force logo on the right ear in teal, a white bow with a tiny teal polka dot bow mounted in the center, and finally some Disney princess socks. Knowing the socks would be perfect, I waited until the morning to suggest my plan. I first mentioned it as Juleah was rolling out of bed after Emma's wake up call.

"We should all wear our socks!" I told her, holding mine up for emphasis.

"To practice?" she asked through a yawn.

"Yeah," I nodded. "I bet if we messaged everyone we could all wear them and match. It would be perfect."

I knew it was a long shot, but wearing socks worked well to cover my ankle for our last practices at the gym so I knew it would be a good way to cover the injury. Thankfully, Juleah quickly agreed, followed by both

Addison and Emma. We buzzed around the hotel room getting our practice uniforms on while also texting other athletes. While everyone else took their time to do their hair and makeup, I pulled my hair into a simple half pony so I could slip on my new bow, then smudged on some chap stick. It wasn't as extravagant as everyone else, but was good enough for me. It also gave me more time to make sure the sock plan was a go for everyone on the team.

"How much time until we need to be down there?" Juleah asked as we were finally leaving our room. We were all dressed alike, complete with teal drawstring bags we received during our trip to Dallas for NCA and lanyards we were required to wear everywhere. The badges attached to the fabric necklace and allowed us entry to the parks all week, so they were definitely important.

"We have an hour I think," I replied, pulling my phone out of the waistband of my cheer shorts. "Yup. 54 minutes to be exact."

"Perfect," Juleah grinned. "Enough time to eat lots of bacon before working hard enough to puke it all up."

"Good outlook," Addison said, although she didn't sound convinced of Juleah's plan.

"I'm just excited to go to the park later," Emma announced.

As we finished our walk to breakfast, we continued to talk about what rides we were excited to go on the most. Sure, we had a long team practice before we could begin our afternoon, but it was an important discussion all the same. Mostly because it was going to be one of the last chances for us to really have fun and relax before competitions began. After we stepped on the stage to perform for the first time, everything would be much more serious and intense. Until then, however, we could act like tourists a little bit.

"Love the socks," Gwen said as we walked into the food court. She was sitting at a table with a few other members of Bomb Squad, all wearing hot pink tank tops with their team name in shiny letters. "We totally should have done that too."

"Did you already eat?" I asked her, noticing there wasn't any food in front of her on the table.

"Yeah, but I think I need a coffee now," she explained.

With that, Gwen stood up and began the walk with me to a nearby counter to place our orders. Like many of the girls from our gym, as well as most of the others in the food court, Gwen had her hair and makeup done to impress. Her brown hair was pulled into a high ponytail to allow her hot pink sequined bow to be featured prominently. Her facial features were enhanced with 'natural makeup,' which I learned was actually done with a lot more makeup than I wore to most competitions. But it went well with her pink clothing and nails. Much like my teal nails, her pink polish helped even more to show her team spirit.

While we chatted, I noticed the large number of other cheerleaders around the room, and all the team colors and logos they were wearing on their practice gear. It was very similar to the atmosphere at competitions, only a lot more laid back. This was largely due to the cheer shorts and tanks that most people were wearing. Not to mention the massive bows that were easy to spot even all the way across the room that were a little less fancy than what most teams wore on the competition floor.

"So has your dad been texting you nonstop since you got here?" Gwen asked. It was common knowledge around the gym that my dad was arriving late to Worlds, mostly since it meant everyone needed to take care of their own snacks until he showed up.

"Not too much," I shrugged. "He's super busy at work so I think that's helping. I have a feeling I'll get a lot of messages tonight to make up for all the time he's in the lab."

"Sounds about right," Gwen agreed.

For some reason the reminder that my dad wasn't there made me think again of my ankle. Mostly since the only texts that I had gotten from him since my flight landed in Florida was reminders to rest and ice my ankle. I had a feeling that if my dad knew it was feeling worse than when I went to the doctor, I would be in big trouble. But, what he didn't know, in this case, would allow me to still attend practice. Which was my main goal, after all.

"Next," the clerk at the counter called out to me.

"Finally," I said with a grin. Then, I stepped forward to order a breakfast filled with bacon and carbs. Bacon wasn't the best choice before a long workout, but after smelling it the second I walked into the food court, I knew I needed to eat some as soon as possible.

CHAPTER 19

"Wow," I muttered, mostly to myself, as I walked with my friends to our practice location.

We were in the large field located at the ESPN Wide World of Sports housing, a space that was decorated to look like a football field. It made sense since cheer wasn't the only sport that came through the area for competitions and things of that nature. But I still couldn't help but mentally correct the designer of the decorations. After all, the cheering we did was much more advanced than what you would see on the sidelines of most high school and even college football games.

"A little overwhelmed Max?" Connor asked. He placed a hand on my back as if to guide me to continue walking. Until then I wasn't even aware I had stopped moving altogether. "It's a lot to take in the first time."

"Yeah, it's a lot alright," I agreed, thankful for Connor guiding me forward.

Knowing I needed to focus on not only where my team was walking but also keeping my ankle injury as unnoticeable as possible, I did my best to stop looking around me. It was hard, but also necessary at the same time. As much as I wanted to see everyone else's routines and bows and everything else, I knew I would have my chance after Worlds. Once Worlds was over I could go back and watch all the footage I wanted online. But first I needed to focus on the moment and do my best to get my team to the finals.

"Do you think TJ's going to make us run?" Emma asked, coming up beside me. "We would have to do like a thousand laps around here to get three miles done."

"He better not," Connor said with a sigh. "It's way hotter here than it was when we left Texas."

"Agreed," Emma replied. She then made a face at her phone, no doubt getting more footage for her vlog.

"Gather around, Nitro," TJ called out before we could continue our conversation about conditioning. "As you can tell we have a bit of company out here today, but we still need to get down to business. Everyone needs to stretch out, especially our fliers.

Then we're going to do some basic warm-ups and start running moves. Let's get moving people."

I nodded, then started stretching, all while keeping my right ankle from pulling or twisting too much. Matthew helped me get the stretches to hyperextend so I would be more than ready to fly, then sat next to me while stretching himself as well. Since he was a base he wasn't as flexible as myself or the other flier, but he would still need to be ready to throw standing jumps like always.

"How's the ankle?"

Matthews' question caught me off guard, but I quickly recovered. "Pretty good," I shrugged. "I might need help taping it better for walking around the parks, though."

"Do you have it taped now?" he asked, raising one eyebrow.

"Kind of," I said slowly. "I had to do it pretty fast though since I didn't want everyone in my room to notice what I was doing. It should be fine though."

"I'll be the judge of that."

I was a little confused by Matthew's words, but simply focused on getting ready to perform. Once we were done with what amounted to a watered down version of our usual conditioning, we went right into warming up our stunts. It was then, with Matthew keeping me in the air by holding onto my right foot, that I started feeling pain worse than anything I had since getting the injury. The normal dull throbbing turned instantly into a shooting pain that began at my ankle and radiated all the way up to almost my knee. It made holding my body position all but impossible. In fact, as the pain grew I began falling back to the ground I had been standing on just moments before.

"You good?" Matthew asked me after catching me by my waist to slow me down in my fall.

"Yeah," I said through gritted teeth. "Let's try it again."

Matthew looked like he was about to correct me, but instead took hold of me one more time. I pushed my legs off the ground after dipping low then was again launched into the air. This time I also bit down on my tongue in an effort to keep from screaming or falling out of the stunt too soon. Despite trying to bite lightly, I could taste blood almost immediately. It was worth it though, since I managed to stay in the air, the pain manageable. Or at least manageable until we started to go over more and more of the routine.

"Max, what's going on with you today?" TJ asked once I missed my double around to extension. The move required me to spin around twice as Matthew, Juleah, and Addison lifted me to stand above their heads at an extension position. Even with Juleah's hands gripping both ankles to help stabilize them, I fell almost immediately after I stood in the final position with my arms locked in a high v formation.

"Uh," I began, knowing I didn't really have a good excuse ready for him.

"All these people watching is a real distraction," Emma said, coming to my rescue. "I can't seem to focus today either."

"Yeah," I agreed. "I feel like everyone is watching us extra close after NCA."

The comment made the look on TJ's face change right away. He went from looking annoyed that I fell out of my stunt, to looking once again bummed about NCA. It was the hardest loss of our season, but over time we realized our lack of focus in the final round was thanks to the hype. All everyone talked about after we left the mat the first day was how shocking it was we did so well, and how the title was "ours to lose." There were so many posts online and people that even came up to us to let us know they would be watching us in the finals that it was like everything made us forget to just live in the moment and focus on what we needed to do in order to win.

"This isn't NCA," he finally said. "It's more important than ever to do everything right and stay focused. Everyone run the stunt again."

Shooting a quick glance back at Matthew I got ready to perform the skill once more. Before I was lifted into the air, I made sure to take a deep breath in an effort to get my emotions totally under control. Or rather to be ready to mask the emotion of pain that was sure to come once I was standing with all my weight on my right ankle.

Knowing that TJ was watching me closely, I channeled all the pain I was feeling into an over the top cheer face. It did little to ease the throbbing I was feeling but gave me something to focus on all the same. Based on the looks Emma, Matthew, and Connor were shooting me through the rest of team practice, I knew I wasn't fooling too many people. In fact, it didn't seem that I was fooling TJ much either. Through the rest of warm ups and then the five full outs we ran, he seemed to keep an eye trained on me. It made the time pass slower than usual, especially when we dropped stunts on our final full out and had to run it all again.

"Circle up people," TJ called out as we finally reached the end of practice. "Today was rough. I think there's a lot of nerves going on, and on top of that, a lot of you aren't focusing. We don't have a lot of time between now and when we get on stage Sunday, so some of you might need to get some extra conditioning and stunt work in tonight." He paused to glance towards where I was standing. "Now I know today is park day for everyone, so I won't add a practice in tonight. But come tomorrow ready to work. And remember everyone needs to wear lots of sunscreen and stay hydrated. Nothing hurts more than doing a dozen full outs with a sunburn."

We all put our hands in and did our standard Nitro team chant before heading our separate ways. I expected TJ to pull me aside, but instead he pulled out his phone and began rapidly typing out messages. Seeing that made me feel like I was off the hook. Or at least until I saw the serious look on my friend's faces. Clearly, they weren't letting me get off easy after seeing how much I had to push through the pain during our practice time. I may have been good at covering things up with a cheer face, but they still saw right through it.

CHAPTER 20

"Spill, now," Emma said the second Juleah and Addison walked out of our room.

"Fine," I replied with a sigh.

I was thankful Emma waited until our roommates left to go get lunch before making me tell her about my ankle. The fewer the people that knew about it the better. Unfortunately, Emma was still making me tell her everything. And I did just that. I let her know about the pain I felt at our last Nitro practice back at the gym, and about the constant throbbing that had only intensified since the practice we had just returned from. Although Emma had only recently learned I was injured, she now knew I'd downplayed the seriousness of it. So, as I finally told her all of the truth her eyes went wide in shock.

"That's so stupid Max," she announced.

"Thanks," I said sarcastically, although I knew she was right.

"If you keep this up you might not be able to perform in finals, not to mention before then," she went on, ignoring my comment.

"TJ doesn't know, so that won't happen," I replied.

"It's not just about him." Emma's words confused me, but thankfully she continued. "The more you push yourself and try to keep working through the injury, the worse it's going to get. It might not be that bad right now, but every time you go full out you're risking an even worse injury. One that might keep you from even walking on it for a while, let alone cheering. Or worse, something that will need surgery, meaning you miss out on this season and maybe even some of next season. As important as performing here is, not making an injury worse is way more key."

"So, I just give up on Worlds and head home?" I knew my voice sounded pretty snotty and even childish, but I couldn't help it. "I've been working for this all season. I can't just give up now."

"I'm not saying you need to give up," she assured me, moving to sit next to me on the bed. "What I'm saying is that you need to be smart about this. Which means you let me wrap it, and actually wear the brace your dad got you. And then you let TJ know it's injured."

"We can't tell him!" I all but shouted.

"We have to tell him something," she quickly went on. "You can say you just noticed it was hurting, or mention it feeling swollen. Whatever. You just need to tell him something. That way when he sees you wearing the brace he knows why, and then if you need to go light on practice tomorrow and Saturday, he won't be mad. In fact, I bet he'll have you mark a lot of the routine so you're definitely good to go on Sunday and for the finals."

I resisted the urge to open my mouth and tell Emma it was a terrible idea, but I couldn't. Her plan made sense. It was a good middle ground between getting help with my ankle while also still getting to downplay everything as much as possible. Not only that, but it would actually allow me to get some rest without counting me out for the performances that really mattered.

"Fine," I finally agreed, causing Emma to wrap her arms around me in a big bear hug.

"Now finish getting ready," she instructed me, holding up her phone. "We have to leave for the park soon."

As Emma began texting, I could only assume with Matthew, I went into the bathroom and finished drying my hair and pulled it up into a half ponytail so I could pop in a bow. I didn't love that I was wearing more gym clothing and a bow after just changing once practice was over, but after experiencing the same thing the year before when I was in Florida for Summit, I was used to it. After grabbing the brace from the bottom of my suitcase, I leaned down to slip it over my foot but stopped after one glance at my ankle.

Not wanting to alert Emma too soon, I moved back into the bathroom and propped my foot up on the closed toilet lid. I then leaned in to get a better look and saw that my ankle was more swollen than ever before. Including right after the initial injury in the backyard and right after I rolled it at Nitro practice. It instantly made me worried, but I tried to tell myself it was going to be fine once I got it better stabilized. Putting on my best attempt at a calm face, I walked out of the bathroom and straight to Emma.

"Can you help me wrap it for more support before I put on the brace?"

"Of course," she grinned, grabbing an ace bandage out of her bag then moving towards me as I sat on one of the beds. After one glance at my ankle, she paused and looked at me. "This looks really bad. Does it still hurt?"

"Only a little," I shrugged, once again lying to my friend. "I just need to elevate it for a while, it's fine."

"Yeah right," Emma said, complete with an eye roll.

Thankfully, she didn't fight with me too much, instead focusing her anger on wrapping my ankle tight enough to keep it supported without cutting off circulation to my toes. I could tell the difference it made immediately, although it was far from a cure. And when combined with my brace, it was feeling almost manageable. I was ready for the park. Or at least I was until I learned that a lot of people were concerned about me putting weight on it all day.

"That's a lot of walking," Nick commented, despite not really knowing the extent of my injury.

"Yeah, maybe you should take it easy," Juleah agreed.

"Really?" I asked, looking around at the other athletes that were standing close to me while waiting on a shuttle to the park.

"I think she'll be okay," Emma shrugged. I wasn't sure if she really meant it, or was trying to downplay the seriousness of the situation as we had planned. "If it starts to hurt more, Connor can just give her a piggy back ride."

"Exactly," Connor grinned, stepping closer to me to wrap an arm around my shoulders.

"Thanks, but I think I'll be okay," I laughed.

"Good, then he can carry me when I get tired," Matthew announced, then made a show of trying to climb onto Connor's back.

The laughter and fun of the moment was just what I needed to take the spotlight off me. Instead of spending even longer talking about my ankle, everyone moved on to talking about what rides they 'needed' to ride, or what food they were most excited to try. All of it got me really excited to spend the day with my team having fun. It was just what I needed to keep my mind off my injury, and also let me relax before I had to face TJ and try to explain to him what was going on.

CHAPTER 21

"How's your ankle feeling this morning?" Juleah asked as we all got dressed and ready on Friday.

"Really good," I replied quickly. I knew she was likely the first of many people who would be asking me the same thing all day. Not to mention it was a question that had been plaguing me for a while now.

My answer seemed to satisfy her, even though it wasn't entirely true. The truth was all the walking made my ankle hurt more and more as the day went on. But, at Emma's insistence, I actually did get a few piggy back rides from Connor. He offered them all day, but it wasn't until Emma noticed me wince while walking up the steps to a ride that she started insisting I accept his offers.

Once we made it back to the resort we went back to our room where I was forced to ice and elevate my leg, although the pain was strong enough I needed no encouragement at that point.

"Do you need help wrapping it again before you put the brace on?" Addison asked as she pulled her frizzy black hair into a high ponytail.

"That would be great."

As Addison sat on her bed across from me wrapping up my ankle, I worked on pulling my hair up. Unlike when it was long, I was able to put it up easily even without a mirror. Instead, I just used my teasing comb and a little hair spray and was good to go. I would need a mirror to get my bow in place, but practice was starting a little later than the day before so I knew I still had plenty of time.

Just as Addison was finishing up with my ankle, the sound of my phone buzzing from across the room caught my attention. Before I could get up to grab it, Emma picked up my phone and tossed it towards me. I caught it easily, then smiled when I saw I had texts coming in from both my dad and Peter. My dad's text was just an update letting me know how many hours were left until he would be heading to the airport, while Peter's message simply said, "Good luck at practice." It felt nice to know they were both thinking of me. And even better than that, it was only a few more hours until my dad would finally be arriving in Florida.

"Alright, time for breakfast?" Emma asked, emerging from the bathroom in her practice uniform and a full face of makeup.

"Yup." After I answered I rushed to the mirror so I could pop my bow in place. It was the same bow as yesterday; the teal bow with the Mini Mouse accent bow from our gift bags. Once I had it secured with a few bobby pins, I grabbed my drawstring bag and phone then followed my friends out into the hot Florida air.

Breakfast was much like the day before, only much more crowded. More and more teams had arrived in the last 24 hours, which meant less open tables and longer lines for food. Even with the later start time for practice, we had to rush to finish eating to make it to where TJ was waiting in time. Thanks to an early morning group text, we arrived at a large open field not far from the area where we had practiced the day before. There were a few other teams around as well, all apparently looking for a place to work on their skills without the other teams watching or distracting them quite so much.

"Hey TJ, can I talk to you?" I asked, approaching him the second I arrived at the practice spot.

"Of course," he nodded. "What's up?"

"My ankle is feeling a little weird," I started, unsure how to word everything

147

despite a long conversation about it with Emma the night before. "I think I landed on it wrong yesterday at some point. It kind of just hurts a bit when I put too much pressure on it."

"We should have it looked at," TJ said immediately, the words I was most afraid to hear.

"I called my dad and talked to him and he thinks it sounds like I just rolled it," I continued. "He said he can look at it tonight, but that it might be good to wrap it and rest it a little if I can. But it doesn't really hurt too much, so I think I'm still okay to practice."

"No," TJ spoke with a firm voice and help up a hand to stop me, making me instantly more nervous. "This morning I want you to rest and elevate it, and then if your dad wants to be the one to look at it tonight that's great. But you're not doing any stunting or tumbling until he gives you the all clear."

"But-"

"No buts," he cut me off immediately. "I know you, Max. You could lose a leg and would still get out there and try to fly on just one leg. That's what I love about you. But I need you good to go for Sunday and Monday. If that means you miss a little practice time today then I'm okay with that."

As much as I wasn't happy to be missing out on practice time, the fact that TJ was making it clear I would be taking the mat with my team when it mattered the most was my main focus. It was like a breath of fresh air knowing that all I needed to do was have my dad give TJ the go ahead and I would be back performing with my team. Or maybe performing wasn't the right word for it, as I soon learned.

"This morning we're doing conditioning," TJ began explaining to the team a few minutes later. "Full conditioning like always, and then some added stunt work and tumbling. Then everyone gets a few hours off before we're back here again. Tonight we're doing a full practice then meeting up with Bomb Squad and Detonators for dinner and a final little showcase. We want everyone to perform for each other and give support before we head into tomorrow."

Tomorrow, as we all knew, was the first day of performing for Detonators. After receiving an at-large bid, instead of their usual full paid bid, they would have to prove themselves before taking the mat Sunday as well as Monday. Bomb Squad and Nitro, thanks to their full paid bids, would have the day to do final practices and also cheer on Detonators and the other teams kicking off the weekend of performances.

The other athletes around me groaned at the thought of conditioning before getting up and starting a few laps around the field. Meanwhile, I sat in the grass and worked on stretching and core workouts. TJ didn't exactly tell me I needed to work on anything while I was skipping the conditioning, but I felt like everyone else on the team needed to see I was putting work in even if I wasn't out there running as well. It made the time pass quickly enough, despite the sun beating down on me. Even just going through the motions of some of the workout from my seat on the sidelines left me exhausted. It made me feel bad for everyone that was working twice as hard as me, but there was little I could do about it in that moment.

"I might need two showers to get all the sweat off," Emma announced as we all made our way back to our rooms once the morning practice was over.

"I might need three."

Matthew made his comment, then made a show of wiping sweat off his forehead that he immediately tried to wipe onto Emma. She let out a yelp, then ran a few steps away from him, their flirty interaction causing the rest of us to laugh. They eventually rejoined us, the running too much to keep up after how much work they had put in at practice. In fact, we mostly walked in silence until we reached the elevators that would take us girls up a few floors while the guys made their way farther down the line of rooms.

"Lunch in the food court in an hour?" Matthew asked, his attention mostly locked onto Emma.

"I might need a nap," she said with a sigh. "We'll text you."

As the two shared a kiss, the rest of us girls climbed into the elevator, instantly feeling even hotter thanks to the confined space. Even with just five of us standing together, it was like the sticky feel and smell of sweat was intensified. We held the door until Emma finally removed herself from Matthew and joined us in the elevator. In doing so, I saw Connor give me a weird look. Before I could ask him what the look was about, the door closed. Thankfully my phone also went off a second later with a text from Connor.

"Make sure you ice and rest that ankle," he wrote. "Performing isn't the same without you, even just at practice."

"He's too sweet," Addison said in my ear, clearly having read the text over my shoulder.

"He just wants to make sure we walk away with those rings," I said simply, while texting Connor back.

"If you say so," Juleah chimed in, then exited the elevator as soon as the door slid open on our floor. "I call shower first."

CHAPTER 22

I would love to say that my dad arrived, took one look at my ankle and told me I was good to go. I would also love to say that this was all thanks to the swelling going down, as well as a lot less pain. But that's not what happened. Not even close.

"This is serious Max," my dad said simply.

After arriving at the resort from the airport, the first thing my dad did was look over my injury. I had texted him that I needed it looked at as soon as I was done showering after the afternoon practice session. That meant the second he was in his room I raced to show him the state of my ankle. Even with resting it all morning, it was still rather swollen. Not to mention when my dad tried to slightly bend it or apply pressure I had to try extra hard not to cry from the sharp pain.

"It's really not that bad," I tried to assure my dad, my voice not confident in the slightest. "I just need to ice it again."

"What you need is to ice it, and then stay off of it for a few days."

"I can't miss Worlds," I reminded him, as if he didn't somehow know the severity of the situation.

"You can miss Worlds, and you will if you don't take care of yourself, sweetie." His face softened then, likely since he knew I wasn't going to go down without a fight. "I understand this is important. I really do. But you need to realize that it can get a lot worse if you keep trying to just push through this."

"Why does everyone keep saying that?" I asked with a roll of my eyes.

"Maybe because it's true?" he asked, although it was clearly a rhetorical question. "Everyone is just trying to look out for you."

"I get it," I began, trying to keep my voice calmer than I was feeling. "I just have to do this. I have to prove to everyone that Nitro can win. After NCA everyone is just waiting for us to fail again, and I can't be the cause of it. Without my tumbling and flying, winning would be next to impossible." When my dad raised an eyebrow, I quickly continued. "I'm not saying I'm the most important person on the team. But I'm still a part of the team. If I can't go out there and perform like I've been doing all season, then I'll be letting everyone down and making all the hard work all season for nothing."

"Not for nothing," he said with a shake of his head. "Nitro had a great season, especially considering everything that happened this summer."

I knew he was referring to the bullying from Leanne I went through as well as the rebuilding the team had to go through to replace her after she was removed from the gym. There were a lot of people that were worried that without her we couldn't make it to Worlds. In fact, there were people that even made comments on social media that without Leanne we were headed for a very disappointing season. But the truth was, we had a great season. We got a bid to Worlds early on, won almost every competition all season, and we all worked extremely hard on gaining new skills. All but a few of the 20 athletes on the team were throwing much harder tumbling passes and flying skills than ever before. Worlds would just be the icing on the cake, but would also be how everyone would remember us next season and the ones to follow.

"If I promise to be really careful can you just tell TJ I'm okay to perform?"

"I'll think about it," he sighed, likely knowing how intense my determination to perform really was. "Until then you need more ice and you need to sit with it elevated."

"Deal," I grinned, then tried to sit still while my dad reapplied the ace bandage and brace. "Did TJ tell all the parents about the team dinner tonight?"

While my dad caught me up on the plan for parents to join all the athletes for both dinner and to watch the performances later I glanced at my phone to check in on the time. I still had an hour until we were all meeting for dinner, but would need to get dressed. When I packed for Worlds I wasn't sure why we were all told to bring a nice outfit, but clearly, the dinner was going to be a little fancier than just pizza in a pavilion. In fact, from the little info we got out of TJ, it sounded like we were going to be heading into town for a nice dinner at a restaurant. It would be a fun way to start the weekend of performances, not to mention the evening of practices and performances as well.

"I better go get ready," I told my dad, standing up once he was done with my ankle. "Thanks Dad."

"For what?" he asked, gesturing to my ankle as if to say it was no big deal.

"For my ankle, I guess," I shrugged. "But also for everything else. Summit was great last year, but Worlds has already been even better. If I didn't have you there last year to remind me how much fun I have at cheer then I might have played softball again instead of staying at TNT Force. So, thanks."

Pulling me into a tight hug, my dad planted a kiss on my forehead before letting me go so I could rush to my room to get ready. As I walked I couldn't tell if my ankle was any better, but this was more than likely because it hadn't been that long that I'd been resting it. Even with sitting out at practice and getting some rest in the hotel room after lunch, it was short compared to how much time I had spent walking and even cheering on my ankle since it first got hurt.

"You need to get dressed fast," Emma announced to me as soon as I walked into our room.

"I have tons of time," I explained, holding up my phone for her to see the time.

"Not quite," she began with a mischievous grin, all of which was being filmed for her vlog.

"Emma's decided you're getting a makeover," Juleah grinned, clearly loving the idea as well.

"Seriously?" I asked, hoping I was wrong. But their facial expressions told me it had already been decided without me. "Addison?"

"I'm with them," she laughed, holding up hairspray and a curling wand for emphasis.

"Why does everyone always want to give me makeovers?" The question was more to myself, but got my friends laughing all the same.

"You can figure it out after you get dressed," Emma said, holding out a dress to me with the hand not holding her phone.

"What's this?" I asked, looking at the mint colored dress dotted with silver and white beading.

"I brought an extra dress," she grinned. "We looked in your suitcase. You can't just wear the dress tonight that you wore to the end of the year banquet. It's basically against the law."

I opened my mouth to fight her, but knew there was no way I was going to win that battle. So, instead, I took the dress and walked into the bathroom to change. Thankfully, the dress was flowy enough that it was pretty comfortable despite the delicate straps and intricate bead work. As much as I didn't like getting dressed up, I knew with my friends helping me, it might be at least a little fun. And, with three of them helping, I knew it was going to go a lot faster than when just Lexi and Halley gave me frequent makeovers at our slumber parties. In fact, it was less than 20 minutes after I walked out of the bathroom before I was being sent to look at their hard work in the mirror.

"Looks good, can we go?" I said quickly, hardly looking in the mirror at all.

"That's it?" Addison asked, looking a little shocked.

"Yeah," I shrugged. Then, thinking about it more I went on. "I mean, it looks really good. I guess I'm just getting used to looking really done up by everyone at the gym. It's still not something I can do on my own, but I'm kind of okay with that."

"Oh yeah," Emma nodded. "Lexi was telling me I need to help you with your eyeliner since she and Halley aren't here to help you."

"Thanks," I laughed. "I can never get it to look like anything at all."

Taking a moment to look in the mirror again, I saw that not only did I have my makeup done in a dramatic way that was noticeable but still not as caked on as cheer makeup, my hair was also done a lot different than how I had even seen it. The curls Addison gave me were a lot looser and flowy than how I used to curl my hair when it was long enough to be pulled back in a ponytail for performances. In a way, everything made me look more mature. Something I was okay with, especially as I was the youngest athlete on Nitro; and all of the TNT Force Worlds teams, for that matter.

"It really does look good," I said turning to my friends. "Now can we leave? I'm seriously hungry."

As if on cue my stomach let out a loud grumble. Clearly, the sandwich and pasta salad at lunch hadn't done the best job at filling me up. Thankfully my friends all agreed they were hungry as well, so we made a quick exit from our room. Now that my latest makeover was done, I could focus on eating and then try to convince TJ I could do a little more of practice than earlier in the day.

CHAPTER 23

"Good morning," Connor said to me, leaning down to give me a hug.

"Does this mean you're feeling better," I asked him, raising an eyebrow at his cheery attitude.

"I don't know what you're talking about," he said simply, then turned to talk to Nick who was sitting on the curb outside of the hotel next to me.

His answer was strange, but I turned my focus back to a text I was sending Halley and Lexi. The night before, despite being by my side for the bus ride to the Cheesecake Factory, at dinner, and then again as we returned to the resort to get ready for practice, Connor barely spoke more than five words to me. At first, I thought I was just imagining things, but as the night wore on, it became more and more obvious that he was just sitting and staring at me. Gwen even noticed it when I mentioned it to her on the walk to our rooms after dinner was over.

"I wonder why he's acting that way," I had told Gwen with a sigh.

"Max, you never fail to make me laugh," she had replied, then turned to walk up another flight of steps to her room.

All of it left me confused, but Connor seemed to break out of the weird mood he was in when we went to team practice. As TJ had mentioned, all three of the TNT Force Worlds teams practiced on their own for a while, then we all came together to perform for each other one final time. All the parents also made it down for the performances, cheering us on as we ran everything as close to full out as we could.

Thanks to my injury I was still marking some of the stunts and tumbling, or in some cases changing my flying so I was favoring my left leg instead. It was a lot for Matthew to get used to as far as changing grips and the way he was turning for different choreography, but we were making progress. The plan was to change as much as we could so I could save my ankle for the tumbling which was harder to change, and also worth a lot of points on the score sheet.

"Bus is here," someone called out, alerting all of us to the shuttle that was just pulling into the parking lot.

I sprang up from where I was sitting and got ready to board the bus that would take us over to the performance arena. Around me, other TNT athletes, as well as cheerleaders from other gyms, stood waiting to head out to either watch cheer or perform. There was a cloud of hairspray and glitter all around me, so when Connor slipped an arm around my shoulders, I was happy to have a friend by my side through the chaos. We even managed to find a seat next to each other on the shuttle, along with a few other Nitro and Bomb Squad members scattered around the bus.

"Are you excited?" Connor asked as the shuttle began heading out of the parking lot. "First time at Worlds."

"I'm already at Worlds, remember," I reminded him.

"Well yeah," he nodded. "But this is a little different. You get to finally see everyone and the stage and all of it. Doesn't that have you even a little excited?"

"Kind of," I said thinking it over as I spoke. "I don't know if it will all really hit me until tomorrow when we head backstage though. If I hadn't been through Summit or even NCA then I might be about ready to pee my pants. But hopefully I'll be okay today."

"Yeah, let's make sure you skip the whole peeing your pants thing," Connor agreed with a laugh.

"I'll try my best."

We continued to joke around for the next few minutes until the shuttle came to a stop and we all climbed onto the sidewalk outside the ESPN Wide World of Sports Arena. I barely had time to take in the scene around the building before I had to start following my fellow TNT Force athletes inside. We scanned our lanyards at the entrance before the staff let us join the large sea of cheerleaders already inside. I saw uniforms and gym names I recognized from competitions all season, as well as many that were brand new to me. It was hard to take it all in while still keeping up with the teal and bright pink clad friends I had arrived with. Knowing I didn't want to lose them for good, I reached out and grabbed Connor's hand.

"I don't want to get lost," I told him when he looked back at me with a strange look on his face. My answer seemed to be good enough, since he simply gave my hand a squeeze and kept walking.

Just when it felt like we had walked around the entire arena, everyone stopped and stepped off to the side of the long corridor. Since we were stopping I dropped Connor's hand, confident I wasn't going to lose anyone while we were standing around talking.

"So, we have almost an hour," Emma was telling people around her. "But some of the teams we go up against start in a few minutes. Do we want to go down closer so we can see Detonators up close or get a spot with some of the team moms up in the higher seats?"

"I want to go down close," I said immediately, knowing that being closer to the mat would make it all feel more real.

"Same," Connor said beside me, followed by a few more people as well.

"I'm going to go find my mom and sit up top if anyone wants to come with me," Layla, a girl on Bomb Squad said, which seemed to make everyone else that didn't want to go down close happy.

"Perfect," Emma finally grinned as everyone appeared to know where they were heading to watch once the Detonators took the stage. "Let's go!"

Grabbing Connor's hand once again, I followed Emma and Matthew and the other people who wanted to sit down closer. Everyone was quite a bit taller than me, so I didn't know where we were going for most of the walking. But, since most of the people I was with had been to Worlds at least once or twice before, I trusted they were getting us to where we needed to be. Thankfully, it was just a few minutes until we walked out of the series of hallways we had been traveling through and into the arena that was pumping loud music through the speakers. The lights were all off in the room, aside from the large stage lights that were aimed at the team in the middle of their routine. We all paused to watch them, not wanting to walk in front of anyone until their performance was over.

Once the girls on stage began heading off the mat we continued walking again, the lights in the front of the room sweeping around in a pretty and dramatic light show. The music from their routine that had ended with the team on stage was replaced with a song I heard on the radio at least three times a day on the way to and from cheer practice. I found myself singing along as I followed my friends, my hand still clinging tightly to Connor's.

"This should work," Matthew finally said, turning around to speak to everyone. After he spoke I watched him turn his gaze to myself and Connor, his eyes instantly growing wide. "Max?"

"Yeah?" I asked, dropping Connor's hand and moving closer to Matthew to hear what he was about to say.

"What was that about?" When I didn't immediately reply, he tried again. "Were you holding hands with Connor?"

"I didn't want to get lost," I said simply, not seeing why he was making such a big deal about it.

Matthew looked like he was going to say something else, but when the announcer began calling the next team to the stage, we all quickly moved to find a seat. I sat down between Gwen and Juleah and then turned my attention to the athletes in black and red that were taking the stage. They were the first of a series of squads performing that were all trying to make it into the next day of competition. Every team had a lot to prove, and while some rose to the occasion, others crumbled under the pressure. Thankfully, Detonators was one of the teams that managed to hit their routine perfectly, putting everyone in a super great mood once their performance was over and we began heading out of the arena.

"Okay, now I'm even more pumped for practice," Juleah said with a grin as we walked out into the main hallway of the arena.

"Same," I grinned, then glanced up and saw a bathroom sign on the wall. "Hey, I'll be right back. Wait for me, okay?"

Not wanting to lose the group I raced into the bathroom and into an open stall. Once I was done I tried to wash my hands as quickly as I could before slipping on my backpack and turning to walk out of the bathroom. But, as I turned around, I stopped short when I saw a familiar face standing in front of me.

"Oh, hey there Max," the girl said to me, her smile more like a sneer as she looked me over. It didn't help that her blue eyes were surrounded by a thick layer of black eyeliner that only made her orange-tan skin and white blond hair look even more over the top. Her expression suddenly looked a lot smugger as she laid eyes on my ankle brace.

"Uh, hi," I replied at a sudden loss for words.

"Good luck this weekend. Looks like you're going to need a miracle to make it to finals."

With that she turned and walked into an open stall, slamming the door behind her. Not knowing what else to do I turned and walked out of the bathroom and towards my friends who were all waiting for me. Once I got to them, they all took off towards the shuttle, causing me to follow blindly while still processing what had just happened. It wasn't until I was sitting on the bus next to Connor again that everything finally seemed to hit me.

"Are you okay Max?" Connor asked, looking concerned at my confused and angry face.

"I don't know," I shrugged. "Leanne was in the bathroom."

"What?" he asked automatically.

"Yeah," I nodded, still not believing myself even as I said the words. "She's at Worlds."

CHAPTER 24

For some reason, seeing Leanne had me feeling uneasy the rest of the day. It was almost like it shook my confidence and made me doubt my ability to go out there and do what I had been working on all season. Sure, my ankle was also trying to stop me from performing the routine like always. But when Leanne implied that I wasn't going to be able to live up to the expectations surrounding Nitro, it had a lot more weight. I tried to brush it off all afternoon, but by the time we met in the field for our evening practice I was feeling more nervous than ever. It didn't help that TJ called me aside before practice began, an intensely serious look on his face.

"Is everything okay?" I asked, a little worried from his facial expression.

"Not really," he said simply. "Why didn't you tell me you got hurt while we were still back home?"

"Oh, that," I managed, despite feeling like everything was falling apart. "Did my dad tell you?"

"That would have been okay actually. But no, not your dad. Tonya told me." Before I could say anything, he continued. "I mentioned your ankle last night when all of us coaches were chatting after the run-throughs and she asked me if it was getting worse. There I was, your coach, clueless to what she was talking about. And imagine how it felt to hear that not only did she know about everything, but that she's known for almost a whole week now."

"I wasn't going to tell her but she figured it out," I explained quickly. "When we went to the salon and spa she noticed my ankle was a little puffy. That's all."

"That's not all," he corrected me. "She told you that you needed to tell me if things got worse. Which means when you told me about everything yesterday it wasn't just a small problem. Was it?" I shook my head. "Why did you do this Max? Why didn't you come and talk to me?"

"I don't know," I sighed. "I guess I was afraid that you would pull me out of the routine and then I would miss Worlds and then Nitro would lose and what everyone said about us all season was true and I would let everyone down and you would be so mad."

TJ stared at me for a minute, as if trying to take in the word vomit I had just sent his way. He just looked at me, making me feel like I was supposed to say something else. But I didn't know what else to say. Instead I just stood there, using all of my self-control to not squirm under his gaze.

"This was a bad idea Max," TJ finally spoke. "But I'm not mad."

"You're disappointed?" I guessed, remembering hearing the phrase from my dad once when I was younger.

"No," he said simply. "Not disappointed either. I'm furious."

"Oh," I mumbled, and could instantly feel the sting of tears in my eyes.

"I understand that you don't want to miss performing this weekend," TJ explained, his tone softening as he spoke. "But your health is important. If you had been taking it easy when we were back at the gym, then things might not be where they are now. We could have gotten you rest and help and you would be good to go. Instead, we're two days from the most important moment of the season, and if you go out there and perform the routine full out you could cause yourself even more damage than what's already been done."

"I'll be fine," I said, trying to convince both of us. "I have to be."

Despite my attempt to keep my emotions under control, my voice cracked when I spoke, giving my tears permission to finally stream down my face. It was like the gravity of my injury combined with what TJ had said to me, as well as seeing Leanne, was just suddenly more than I could handle. The tears made me feel like I was being childish, but TJ clearly didn't agree. Instead he stepped forward and wrapped me in a hug, something not to be taken lightly.

Since joining the gym I had gotten to know all of the coaches and gym staff pretty well. Tonya was like a big sister, always there for me and the other girls in the gym. Nicole was tough as nails, but cared about everyone more than they could ever know. Lenny and Greg were the kind of coaches that would all but throw a party every time someone landed a new skill and seemed to always have time to work on extra practices when someone asked.

But TJ had a reputation all his own. He was known for yelling, and shouting, and making at least a few people cry every season. It wasn't that he was mean, just tough. It helped that he was also known for being funny and silly when everything was going as it should. Combined, the two sides made him a great coach, but not really the most comforting person. In fact, even after being on Nitro for the whole season, I had only received a few hugs from him, and usually only in celebration after winning competitions. All of that made the embrace even more important.

"You don't have to be strong and do this on your own Max," TJ said, his arms still wrapped around me. "We're a team remember? And the whole team is going to make sure you get through this, okay?"

"Okay." As TJ finally let go of me, I quickly wiped my face, trying to cover any signs I had been crying. "But how?"

"Well, first of all, by not keeping secrets," he explained. "I need you to tell me everything that's happened with your ankle so we can figure out what's really going on."

Knowing it was time for the truth, I spilled everything to TJ. I told him about how I got hurt to begin with, how I injured my ankle again at practice, and also the pain I had felt while running the routine since we arrived at Worlds. He listened to it all without even interrupting to tell me how stupid I had been along the way. Then, when I was done, he turned to the team with a very determined look on his face.

"Alright everyone," TJ announced, gesturing for me to take a seat with the team. "We have a lot of work to do. Max is injured and we need to change up some of the routine so we can prevent further injuries while still getting the most out of the score sheets. Any questions?"

"I have one," Emma announced. "Can Max still tumble at all with her ankle hurt the way it is?"

The question seemed to pause TJ in his tracks, but only for a second. "Considering how long she pushed through without telling everyone she was hurt, I'm not too worried about her. We can leave tumbling up to her, but for now, we need to get the flying and pyramid changed enough that we can lessen the strain on her as best we can."

I was expecting everyone to groan at the thought of more work on choreography, but instead, everyone got to work right away. Thanks to the changes we had made the day before, there wasn't a lot of the routine left to alter aside from pyramid. As the front and center flier for that whole section of the routine, I had an important role to play that would involve a lot of changes to keep my ankle safe.

"Maybe I can try it from a toe touch to a heel stretch?" I asked after the bases under me set me back on the ground. We had just tried to do a skill where they tossed me up for a toe touch before I was caught in a cradle then quickly lifted so I was standing on two feet with my arms in a high v. Since I was coming down with a lot of force, there didn't seem to be a way for them to catch me then lift me without applying way too much pressure and strain to my ankle.

"We can give it a try, but you need to be ready to grab both of them for the back toss and the fly over," TJ replied, waving his arms about wildly while speaking. Thankfully I knew exactly what he meant instantly.

"Alright, set back up," Matthew announced, calling everyone back into action.

Just like that, I walked to the back of the area we were performing in and stood with my stunt group around me. They held onto my ankles so when TJ counted us in they lifted me in the air while spinning me around twice. By the time I was being held above their heads I was holding my right leg next to my head with my left arm, and holding my right arm out to the side so it crossed in front of my leg in a move called a bow and arrow. My group then walked me forward until I could hold onto Lilly's hand in time to be tossed up and forward while still holding the skill. I tucked my body around in a flip despite still holding the bow and arrow, and landed in the arms of another group of bases who were waiting to catch me. Moving my body around until I was crouching with my legs crossed in their arms, I counted the beats until I spun around twice as I moved to a full standing position. Lilly and Emma were on either side of me, and each held their leg closest to me out so I could hold their feet in my hands while they each held onto the foot of a flier that was also being held as a part of the pyramid position. The result was an elaborate multi-level pose that was not only entertaining but also a requirement of the routine.

We had a second to catch our breath before Stephanie and Mary, the two fliers farthest away from me, folded forward out of the pyramid while I let go of the feet I was holding and dropped to be held by my bases at their waist level. After some dramatic arm movements that went with the music that would be playing during our performance, the group holding me tossed me up so I would perform a toe touch while I was high above the mat. As soon as I was caught in a cradle position by my team I found my footing before being lifted into the air while spinning around once and then reaching a full extension position above their heads. As I spun, I also kicked my right leg up to hold the heel stretch position so no one else was touching or jostling my ankle. Or rather that was the plan. Instead, I got halfway up and began to lose my balance. Pitching to my side, I was easily caught before TJ stopped the rest of the athletes around me.

"That was good," he called out once everyone was out of the air and back on the grass. "We might need to take out the twist on the way up after the toe touch. Let's have just Max's group run that part a few times. Everyone else stay close to spot in case she takes a tumble."

Everyone moved quickly, then TJ counted down to try it once again. I knew it was just the start of a long night, but I also couldn't help but smile. It was all coming together.

CHAPTER 25

The evening stretched on and on, but thankfully everyone seemed more determined than ever to get the routine ready for Worlds. I felt bad that I was making everyone else work even more than usual, but considering that they often got to take breaks while I ran the same section of the routine over and over again, no one complained. Instead, everyone stayed focused until we were able to land the pyramid as planned and make some small changes to the dance sequence so I could skip some of my floor work in that section and instead focus on my final basket toss.

"So, do we still have a shot?" I asked TJ between long drinks of water once we were dismissed to finally head to dinner.

"I think so," he said with a grin. "If you can still get some of your more basic tumbling in then I think we should be good. But right now, you need to go ice and elevate that ankle and take some ibuprofen. You need to rest your ankle every second you can get."

"Got it," I nodded, then turned to walk back to my room.

"Oh, and Max," TJ called out, getting my attention easily. "I'm not happy you didn't tell me sooner, but I'm still really proud of you. This is Nitro's year. I can feel it."

His words stayed with me the rest of the evening as I hung out with the team at the pool, my leg in the hot tub the whole time, and then again as I woke up the next morning and began getting ready to perform. It was time for Nitro to prove once and for all that we were world champions, something I had thought about all season. All of a sudden, it was real. I was literally just two days away from finding out if all the hard work over the last few months was worth it. But first, I needed to make it through performing twice despite my still swollen ankle.

"I need help with my eyeliner," I said with a sigh from where I was sitting on the floor in front of the full-length mirror.

"I'm on it," Emma laughed, moving to sit next to me as I turned to face her.

"Where's your eyeshadow, you need help with that too."

I wanted to tell her my makeup was fine, but I knew she was way better at cheer makeup than me. So, I simply handed her my whole makeup bag and sat patiently while she fixed the work I had already done. As expected, it was done in no time at all and looked even better than when Lexi or Halley helped me do it in the past. I made a mental note to get some lessons from Emma so I could be a little more independent when it came to putting on my makeup, but that could wait.

"We need to head down to breakfast if we're going to get the shuttle on time," Addison said as she stuffed her cheer shoes into her glittery teal backpack.

Glancing at my phone I saw she was right and that we had less than an hour until we needed to meet with TJ and the other members of Nitro so we could watch Bomb Squad. From there we would need to get ready and head into warm-ups. After shoving all of my makeup back into its bag, I quickly moved my uniform bag, cheer shoes, and makeup into my backpack before zipping everything up and slipping on the shoulder straps. Thinking it through again, I took off my bag and quickly added the bottle of ibuprofen that was sitting on the nightstand before slinging it onto my back.

"Okay, I'm ready to go," I announced, then moved next to Addison who was standing by the door. In another minute, we were joined by Emma and Juleah, and the four of us headed quickly to the food court.

"I don't know if I can actually eat anything," Juleah said as we walked. "I'm starting to get nervous already."

"Then you need to eat," Emma told her simply, all while filming on her phone. "You have to eat now so if you get so nervous you puke later the food has at least a little time to get into your system."

"Alright then," Addison laughed. "That's reassuring."

"I only know because it happened to me my first year at Worlds," Emma explained. She was also laughing with us, clearly aware of how crazy she sounded in that moment. "My friend Erin made me eat all kinds of stuff with protein in case I really did puke, and it was a life saver. I threw up three times during warm-ups, but still had something in me so I didn't faint or anything. I just drank a bunch of Gatorade and went out there and tried to perform like always."

"Well, I don't want to throw up today," Juleah sighed. "I just also don't want to mess up."

"Same," I nodded. "I feel like if I mess up then I let down everyone on the team."

"Not true," Emma corrected me. "Nitro is a team. We win together and we lose together. Simple as that."

"Okay, so you guys won't be mad at me, but everyone else will be making some fairly rude comments," I paused, not sure if I should continue. "Leanne's already saying stuff in fact."

"What?" Juleah asked, actually stopping on the sidewalk to turn and face me. Beside her, Emma stopped filming immediately. "Is she posting things online again?"

"Uh... no." I was surprised by the shocked and almost angry looks my friends were giving me, but knew they were just looking out for me. "I ran into her yesterday in the bathroom after we watched Detonators. She made it sound like her team is going to crush us."

"That's impossible," Emma said with a laugh then began walking once again.

"How are you so sure?" Addison asked as we all rushed to catch up with Emma.

"Because you can't win with a team that doesn't exist." When no one responded, Emma continued. "Hanna from Bomb Squad is good friends with Leanne's cousin Whitney, and Whitney said that after Leanne was kicked out of the gym she couldn't find another team to join. No one wants to take her in after what she did to Max. So she tried for a few months but no one wants her and now she's begging her parents to move or let her go live with her aunt in California so she can join a gym there."

"Wow," I said, not sure how else to put into words how I was feeling.

"She was trying to psych you out for sure," Emma explained. "But she doesn't know what she's talking about. Even with an injury you're better than most of the fliers and tumblers in our division. I'm not worried at all."

Although I didn't feel quite as confident as Emma, I was feeling at least a little better about everything. Knowing that I wasn't going to be running into Leanne while I was backstage warming up was a good thing, even if it meant she was likely still in the audience. But, that was a small thing that I didn't need to worry about. Instead, I focused my energy on chowing down as many scrambled eggs and pieces of bacon that I thought my body could handle. It was a lot of food, but I knew I had a little bit for everything to digest before I needed to start warming up and take the stage.

When we finally arrived at the arena after our late breakfast, I was shocked to see even more people than the day before. Thousands of cheerleaders and their friends and families were making their way in and out of the building, taking photos anywhere they could, and generally giving me butterflies. The moment I had been dreaming of all season had finally arrived and I was more excited than I thought possible.

"How are you feeling today?" Connor asked me once we found the rest of Nitro. We were at a predetermined meetup spot outside the entrance that TJ had chosen.

"My ankle's a little less swollen so that's good," I explained, not bothering to mention my nerves. "As long as I ice it as soon as I'm off the mat, I think I should still be okay to throw all of my tumbling today."

"Don't push yourself too hard," Matthew warned me, having overheard my comment to Connor. "Depending on what the other teams are throwing out there, we might not need all of that today. I mean, today's only worth 25% of our final score, so if you can't tumble full out both days, tomorrow would be the better day to throw everything."

I nodded, knowing Matthew was right. If I played it a little safe and in doing so gave my ankle a break, I would have a better chance of landing all of my tumbling when it mattered most: in the finals. But, at the same time, if I played it too safe, there was always a chance we wouldn't make it to the finals at all. The chances were pretty slim since we knew our routine had a lot of points thanks to our hard pyramid and also our elite stunt sequence. But crazier things had happened at Worlds before. Especially in small co-ed level 5, a division filled with teams that were known for winning year after year.

"Alright people, listen up," TJ called out, getting everyone's attention. "We go back for warm ups in just over an hour. Between now and then we're going to head in and cheer on Bomb Squad. We'll also have a chance to watch Detonators later today. But for now, let's get in there and find our seats."

As TJ turned and began leading the team inside, I could feel the butterflies in my stomach getting worse. Even after being in the arena the day before, suddenly walking into it this time was different. Maybe it was the sea of athletes also wearing their Nitro tank tops and bright teal cheer bows. Or maybe it was the cheerleaders around us from other teams glancing our way as if to size up their competition. Whatever the reason, I knew the hour until we headed to warmups was going to be an unbearably long one.

CHAPTER 26

After watching Bomb Squad perform a flawless routine, I headed to the bathroom with some of the other girls on Nitro to put on our uniforms. As I slipped on the black, teal, and lime green material, I could feel my butterflies from earlier leaving. Instead I felt surer of myself than ever before. I was determined to get out there and prove to everyone watching that I was good enough for the Worlds title, injury and all.

"We have five minutes," Emma said as she sprayed one more layer of hairspray over her curls.

I nodded, then quickly pulled my lipstick out of my makeup bag. It was the one makeup item I could do without help, only because it was the easiest. Knowing it was something I still might mess up, I took my time so the long wear bright red lip color didn't smudge onto my skin at all. Even with the extra effort spent on the application, I was done within seconds and had time to take a step back and look at myself in the mirror.

Two years ago, I never would have recognized myself now. My hair was teased into a front poof surrounded by a massive teal bow, I was wearing layer upon layer of makeup, and the team uniform I was wearing didn't have a number on the back like all the ones I'd worn in the past. Instead my uniform was flashy, sparkly, and showed my entire stomach. A stomach that was tanned and toned thanks to lots of long training sessions in the gym. With NITRO across my chest and a bomb on my hip to represent the TNT Force gym, I may not have looked like the old me, but I felt just as confident as I ever had on any soccer field or softball diamond.

"Ready?" Emma asked once she was finished with her hair.

"Yeah," I nodded. "Let's do this."

As much as I was ready to take the stage, we still had to get through warm-ups. After not tumbling for the last two days, I knew it was going to be my first chance to really see how my ankle would hold up on the mat. I wasn't worried about my baskets, my flying skills, or even the new pyramid we had been working through just hours before. My focus was only on warming up my tumbling.

"Take it easy Max," TJ said to me when I finally walked towards the running tumbling track.

I nodded, then tried my best to shut out everyone else around me. I bounced in place on the mat a few times, then did a round off to get started, feeling only a little sting on the landing. It gave me confidence that I could push through the routine, so I got set up again and this time added in a back hand spring after the round off. As if it was more used to the feeling of landing, my ankle barely reacted when my feet hit the ground. It was all I needed to really go for everything. Shaking my wrists and body out as I walked to the start of the mat, I completed the round off followed by two back hand springs and a whip before flipping my body one last time while also completing two full twists in the air. The double full was a real test for me since it was one of the moves that caused my injury in the first place.

When my feet hit the ground, I could feel the jolt of pain shoot up my leg, but I was able to stay standing. I also made sure to keep the pained expression off my face. If TJ or any of my teammates saw me react, then my tumbling passes would be even more watered down. It wasn't something I was willing to risk, so as I turned towards everyone I made sure to give them a big smile.

"Not bad Max," TJ grinned as Nitro athletes celebrated around him. "Now get out of the way so Matthew can go."

"Beat that," I said to Matthew, then did a dramatic walk off the tumbling track. To everyone else, I knew it looked like I was just being silly, but I knew the truth. The pain was still throbbing in my ankle and stepping all my weight on it wasn't going to be a good idea so soon after landing the double full.

"Do you think you have a few more of those in you?" TJ asked as I finally reached him.

"Yeah," I said with as much confidence as I could muster. "But I don't want to push it too much."

"My thoughts exactly," he nodded. "Just throw whips on the dead mat. And keep it simple here too. We don't want to push you too far too fast."

"If you say so," I said with a sigh, although I was more than thankful. The stabbing pain was slowly getting better, but there was no way to be sure if it was going to fully subside fast enough. Or rather no way to be sure until our names were being called to take the mat.

"Up next in our Small Senior Coed Level 5 division, from Wichita Falls, Texas, TNT Force Nitro."

As the words of the announcer was met with cheers from the crowd I stepped onto the blue mat, a smile plastered onto my face. I jogged forward, my pinky fingers hooked onto Emma to my right, and Lilly to my left. It was how the fliers on Nitro always entered the mat. Mary and Stephanie were also holding pinkies on the other side of Emma, all of us in a line. Then, after Emma, who was in the center of the line, counted to three, we all kicked our right legs high then pivoted as we brought them back to the ground so our legs were in front of the person to our right. It was a rather basic movement as far as on the mat handshakes were concerned, but it was the best way for all of us fliers to be involved in the same thing.

Letting go of both pinkies I had been holding, I moved to give Connor a hug then used both hands to give Juleah a double high five. Once all of it was finished, I moved into my starting spot and waited for the familiar music to start our routine. I could feel each second passing by as I stood there, but did my best to shut out the screaming crowd, the cameras and lights that were trained on me, and the judges waiting to tick off points for every stumble, fall, or small mistake. None of that mattered. All that mattered was ignoring my ankle and any pain that would flare up as I began the 2-and-a-half-minute routine. It was, after all, the only thing between Nitro and the finals.

"Tick, tick, tick, Nitro's going to explode," the voice on our music called out to indicate the start of the routine. I lifted my head so I was no longer looking down at the mat, giving everyone watching a big smile. Then, just as the word explode was spoken I landed a standing full, the first of many I would need to throw in the routine. When my feet hit the mat, I could feel my ankle protesting the movement, but ignored it as best I could. I knew there was a chance I would regret it later, but nothing could stop me from performing like always.

CHAPTER 27

"You need more ice," Connor noted, pointing to the watery Ziploc bag sitting on top of my ankle. "Want me to go get you a refill?"

"I need to keep ice off of it for a little while anyways," I shrugged, leaning to pull the bag aside.

"I'll get that," he offered, clearly still wanting to do something to help.

Before I could tell him it could wait, Connor leaped up and grabbed the now dripping bag of ice. He took it in the direction of the bathroom to no doubt empty it into the sink. I didn't bother watching him go though, since when he got up he left the blanket he was using free for the taking. I quickly grabbed it and draped it over myself, certain to cover my ankle that was still cold from the ice that had just been on it seconds before.

Around me, other members of Nitro, Detonators, and Bomb Squad sat watching the big screen TV in the living room of the suite that TJ and Scott, the coach of Detonators, were sharing. The massive space had two couches, an armchair, and lots of floor space perfect for all of us to camp out and enjoy a movie. Two bathrooms and two bedrooms were also a part of the massive suite, but weren't being used for our little get-together. We were watching animated Disney classics, which was apparently a Worlds tradition. Currently, *Beauty and the Beast* was dancing across the TV screen.

"Hey," Connor frowned when he returned to his seat next to me. "You stole my blanket."

"I don't see your name on it," I said a super childish voice, then took it even further by sticking my tongue out at him.

"First place sure has gone to your head," he laughed, then settled back into his spot, minus his blanket of course.

The mention of first place had me grinning once again. Despite my ankle feeling like it was on fire and ready to drop off my leg by the time we left the mat, Nitro hit a perfect routine. It was an amazing feeling, which only got better when we got our scores and saw we were at the top of our division. The news made me feel like I was back to perfect health since most of my kick doubles were watered down to a kick single while I was on the mat. It meant that even without throwing my usual tumbling passes, we were in a spot to take the Worlds title once and for all.

We, of course, had to keep in mind the fact that two of the teams that were favorites in our division walking into the week had stunt falls. They were small enough mistakes that they still easily made it into the finals, and with that came Nitro's risk of losing. Any one of the teams that had bobbles or errors on day one could come back and win it all if they hit a clean routine on day two when the points were even higher. Which also meant we needed to hit our routines clean again if we wanted a chance of landing in the top three, let alone first.

"Is that Lexi or Halley?" Connor asked, looking over my shoulder as I typed out a long text on my phone.

"Both," I said simply, before adding a few emojis and hitting send. "They've been texting me nonstop since they watched our performance earlier."

"Well, you get to see them tomorrow, right?" he asked.

"Nope," I frowned. "They were going to leave tomorrow like we all did last year, but aren't coming until Wednesday now. Apparently missing so much school isn't working out as well this time around. But, I'll get home early enough Tuesday night that I'll get to see both of them before they leave for Summit."

"I feel like you mentioned that at some point," he nodded. "But my mind has been so focused on Worlds that I can't seem to concentrate on too much else."

"Same," I agreed easily. "It's kind of weird to think after tomorrow the whole season is over and we all just move on."

"Some of us more than others," Matthew said from where he was sitting on the other side of Connor.

"Oh yeah, I almost forgot." I found myself instantly sad as I looked over at Matthew, the reality of everything sinking in a little bit more. "Aren't you going to miss the gym?"

"Of course," Matthew answered instantly. "But I don't leave for UT until August, so in the meantime, I'll be at every tumbling class, stunting class, and open gym so I can get everyone else ready for next season, even if I won't be there."

"Don't remind me," Emma warned Matthew. She was sitting a few feet away with Liz and Jade, but still heard Matthews' comment. "It's not going to be the same next year without you. Or Stephanie and Kate and everyone else leaving."

As the conversation around me continued, I felt conflicted. Sure, I was excited for next season since there was a chance for Halley and Lexi to be on the same squad as me once again, but it also meant saying goodbye to so many people. In total, six of the 20 athletes on Nitro would be leaving the gym thanks to 'aging out,' or basically graduating high school. Combined with a few athletes thinking about moving to either Bomb Squad or Detonators, it meant Nitro would be a totally different team in just a few weeks.

"Well, the season's not over yet," I finally said, a reminder to myself as well as the others around me. "We can deal with being sad after we all win tomorrow."

"Not to be cocky or anything," Emma said with a laugh.

"I'm not being cocky," I assured her, although I couldn't help but smile. "I'm just being confident. I mean, all three teams hit perfect today, and Detonators hit perfect yesterday too. We're clearly making this our year."

The comment instantly got everyone talking, and before I knew it, we were pausing the movie marathon to once again watch through the three routines from the day. We often watched our performances back during the first practice after competitions and videos of full outs while we were back in the gym. It allowed us to see what changes we needed to make, how certain parts of the routines looked, and also helped us understand what we were doing that really worked. And based on the videos of all three TNT Force teams, there were a lot of things working perfectly.

The new section of Nitro's pyramid was the part that I was the most impressed with. Despite changing so much of it to try and not put stress on my injury, it still looked great on the mat. All the little details worked together to make a dynamic and really difficult section of the routine. Which was something we were hoping would also help us in the final round. Between the tumbling and harder elements in the pyramid, it all made for a raw score that any team would have to work hard to beat, as proven by our current first position.

"Okay, I think it's about bedtime," Tonya finally announced after we had watched all three routines before finishing the rest of *Beauty and the Beast*. "Tomorrow's a big day for everyone and I want you all well rested. Lights out is in half an hour, and we will be checking."

"I think she's serious," Connor said to me as we all began to stand up and make our way to the door.

"Of course she is," Emma laughed. "With all of our teams hitting perfect today, we can't risk messing up tomorrow because of something lame like being too tired."

"So true," I nodded. "Although I don't know if I'll be able to fall asleep even if I want to. I'm still a little too excited after our performance earlier."

"Try counting cheer bows," Juleah offered. "It always makes me fall asleep."

"Cheer bows?" Both Connor and Matthew asked at the same time.

"Yeah," she nodded. "It's like counting sheep only way more fun since they're glittery and there's way more bows in the world than sheep."

"Are you sure about that?" Emma challenged her.

"You've seen my bow collection, right?" Juleah asked, as if that would prove her point. Instead, it got both girls going back and forth trying to figure out who between the two of them had more bows.

"If you can't fall asleep and need someone to talk to tonight my phone will be on," Connor said to me, quiet enough that no one could hear it over Emma and Juleah's conversation.

"Thanks," I smiled. "I just might take you up on that one."

When it was finally time to part ways with the guys, I saw it was just after 11, meaning there was technically only one hour until it was officially the final day of Worlds. Even thinking about it made me nervous and anxious at the same time. So, as soon as I got back to the room and changed into my pajamas I pulled out my phone and sent a text to Connor. It wasn't a sure-fire way to help fall asleep, but was my only option as even the thought of finals had me filled with energy and nowhere close to falling asleep.

CHAPTER 28

"Come on in," my dad's voice called out. I pushed on the door after I saw it was left open a little, likely because my dad knew I was on my way. He had, after all, sent me a text asking me to stop by before I was heading to the arena with my team.

"Morning," I grinned, happy to see my dad was wearing his latest cheer dad shirt. It was teal like his last one, only with 'Proud Cheer DAD' embroidered on the front with sparkly silver thread. It was the first day he was unveiling it after purchasing it from a vendor in the Worlds arena.

"Are you sure you have time?" he asked in reply. "You look like you're leaving any second."

"We did a late breakfast instead of trying to fit in a normal lunch before we head over, so we got ready a little early," I explained. "We don't need to be on the shuttle for at least an hour."

"Perfect." He took a seat on the bed and patted the spot next to him. I took the hint and quickly sat down as well. "I have something for you, and well. I just… Just here you go."

As a research scientist, my dad was one of the smartest guys I knew. He knew everything about everything, and was someone people loved to be around. Not just because he was so smart, but also because he was a nice guy and really funny when he wanted to be. But the one thing I never saw him as in my life was nervous. When my mom died he was sad, but even during the hardest moments he never stumbled over his words or struggled to explain to me how he was feeling or what he was going through. So, when he awkwardly handed me a small pink box and a white envelope, I was confused, to say the least.

"What is this?" I asked simply.

"Just take a look," he mumbled, then actually stood up to watch. He was wringing his hands and almost bouncing on the balls of his feet. In any other circumstance, I would have laughed at how strange he was acting, but in that moment I felt the nervousness he was clearly showing.

"But what-"

"Open it," he said simply, pausing his bouncing and moving altogether, as if to emphasize his point.

I wanted to stop and demand that he needed to tell me what was going on, but instead set the box in my lap and opened the envelope. I had a feeling all of it was a gift from my dad, likely something he had also picked up while he was hanging out with the other parents before and after Nitro performed. So, when I looked down at the paper I had pulled out and unfolded from the envelope, I was shocked to see my mom's handwriting.

"My sweet daughter. Although I don't know the exact moment that led to today, I want you to know that I am proud of you. Even without knowing just what it was that you accomplished, I am certain that if I was there in person, I wouldn't be able to stop from wrapping my arms around you in the biggest hug possible. I wish more than anything that I could be there in person to celebrate with you, but know that I miss you and care about you always. I love you Maxine, Mom."

By the time I was done reading my eyes were overflowing with tears, all running down my face and likely taking my eyeliner and glitter along with them. None of that mattered. All that mattered was reading her words for a second time, then finally setting the paper aside to open the small pink box. The box was a flat square, held shut with a small black loop of stretchy string. I pulled the string aside then removed the lid to reveal a thin silver chain with two small silver letters hanging on display. Signs of the hug and kiss my mom couldn't give me in person, the X and the O that hung from the chain made me somehow even more emotional than I already was after reading her note.

"Dad, how did you-" I cut off my words, unable to form a sentence through my still falling tears.

My dad was no longer bouncing or antsy in any way. Instead, he stood with tears running down his face as well. Once I looked up at him he moved to sit next to me, wrapping his arms around me as both of us just held one another and cried. I knew my tears were mostly sad that my mom wasn't there, but I also was feeling a little bit of happiness to have something from her despite how long it had been since she had died. After we sat for a few minutes my dad finally spoke, his voice still heavy with emotions.

"When your mom got sick she wanted to do something special for you," he began slowly. "She knew she was going to miss so many great moments in your life. So she came up with the idea to find little ways to still be there for you. This one was for a moment when you accomplished something big. And as much as I wanted to give this to you later today after you win Worlds, I knew your mom would want you to have it now."

"But what if I don't win today?" I asked, trying to wipe away some of my tears without taking all of my makeup off as well.

"That doesn't matter," he said simply. "You're hurt, but you still went out there and did your best when your team was counting on you. As much as winning today will be a big accomplishment, you're going out there and giving it your all is just as important as winning ever will be."

"Are there more of these?" I asked, holding up the envelope.

"Yes," he nodded. "But that's all I can really say. Your mom told me I wasn't allowed to do anything but give them to you when the moments felt right. This one she wanted me to set aside for a moment when you did something that would have made her proud. I've almost given it to you a dozen times since you joined the gym, but I'm glad I waited until today."

"Me too," I smiled, then gave my dad another hug as more tears began making their way down my face. "I wish she was here."

"So do I sweetie," he agreed before planting a kiss on my forehead.

We sat like that for a few minutes, just sitting together as we both thought about my mom and how much we missed her. Nothing would ever take away the pain of missing her, but knowing that little gifts or notes might be coming to me along the way was a nice surprise I didn't expect when my dad texted me to come to his room to start my day.

"You need to get moving if you're going to get to that shuttle in time," my dad finally said as he slowly let me go from his long embrace.

"Thank you Dad," I said, although I felt like I needed to say so much more at the same time.

"You're welcome sweetie. I'm so proud of you, and I know if she was here, your mom would be just as proud as I am."

Knowing I needed to get back to my room, I gave my dad one final hug before grabbing the envelope and box and finally walking out of the room. The emotions were still heavy as I walked, but the sadness was definitely being taken over by my joy at having the necklace to wear when I was on stage. It would be a small way to feel like my mom was with me as I performed, and that was the best gift I could ever have asked for.

"What happened?" Emma asked as soon as I walked into my room a few moments later.

"Are you okay?" Addison also asked, giving me a worried look from where she stood in the bathroom curling her hair.

"I'm good," I nodded, wiping fresh tears from my face. "My dad gave me a note from my mom. And this."

Overcome with emotions once again, I handed my friends the envelope and box as I moved to grab tissues to wipe up my face. All three girls gave me big hugs between trying to understand what was happening. I had to take breaks as I explained everything to them, still struggling to get a handle on my tears.

"I'm so happy for you Max," Juleah grinned, wiping tears from her own eyes as well once I had finally caught them up on the gift from my mom.

"Same," Addison agreed.

"I'm happy too," Emma finally said. "But before we miss that shuttle we need to get moving. And bring all your makeup. We have a lot of work to do."

Emma gave me one final hug, then I got to work grabbing everything I needed and loading up my cheer bag. I caught a quick peek in the mirror and saw that there was very little of my makeup left, most of it smudges and lines down my cheeks. I tried to wipe some of it off so I would be ready for the second attempt at getting me ready for cheer, but knew I would still look a little bit off until my friends gave me some help. Knowing makeup could wait a minute, I put the necklace around my neck before tucking the note into my bag. I may not have known how the day would end, but what I did know was that everything would turn out much better thanks to the surprise gift from my mom.

CHAPTER 29

With the help of my friends, I was looking more like my normal self by the time we headed back into warm-ups. By that point, everyone on Nitro knew about the necklace and note from my mom, and many of them also seemed emotional when I explained it to them. It didn't help that I managed to get choked up every time I retold the story. But it was a good choked up, a feeling of happiness at having a reminder of my mom with me for Nitro's final shot to win Worlds.

"You got one last performance in that ankle of yours?" Matthew asked, standing next to me as we waited to finish warming up our running tumbling.

"Of course," I assured him. "We just have to do everything exactly how we did it yesterday."

"Exactly the same or are you going to try to throw kick doubles to make sure our score is even better?"

I simply shrugged, knowing that Matthew knew me well. Especially since his words were right in line with my thoughts. From the second I stepped off the mat the day before, I had been trying to decide if throwing the harder tumbling skills was worth it. I wanted to land it to show the world I could do it, and also so I could help my team. But, even doing the double full the day before was proving to be a lot of stress on my ankle. Pushing it more could be pushing it past the breaking point. Literally.

"Let's see it Max," TJ called out, alerting me to the fact that it was time for me to warm up my tumbling.

Stepping onto the long spring loaded mat, I took a few running steps before slamming both feet down and flipping forward in a punch front. The landing was hard, but I knew I needed to push forward. I followed it with a round off and then a move that was even newer to me than the kick double. Performing a similar motion to a back tuck, I moved my body in a half twist so I was now facing the opposite direction from when I began the skill. Known as an Arabian, it allowed me to continue the tumbling pass with another round off before trying a whip and finally a kick full.

My plan had been to throw a kick double, but as I was flying through the air I knew I didn't have quite enough momentum and height off the mat. So, thinking fast I only completed one rotation after kicking my leg up in order to plant my feet back on the mat. Once they hit the mat, however, I could again feel the sharp pain in my ankle, this time much worse than ever before. I tried to keep my face a mask of calm, but as I pitched backward I landed on the very edge of the tumbling track before falling even further back and onto the hard cement floor. The landing didn't hurt my bottom or back at all, mostly because the stabbing pain I was feeling in my leg wasn't subsiding at all even after I was no longer putting weight on it.

"Max!" someone called out, followed by a few more people saying my name or asking if I was okay.

"Don't move, just relax," TJ said to me, after racing to my side. It wasn't until he spoke that I realized I was crying. "I need you to breathe, Max. Nice deep breath."

"Should I get ice?" I heard a voice ask, possibly Connor or Matthew.

"Maybe," TJ answered, his eyes still locked on me. "What hurts Max?"

"My. Ankle." I took a short breath between each word as I still struggled through the intense pain. "It hurts."

"Does your back hurt at all?" TJ asked again.

"No," I said with a shake of my head. "Just my ankle. I think I broke it."

As soon as the words were out of my mouth I could see athletes around me reacting. They were standing far enough away to "give me air" as someone had suggested as TJ was approaching me. But everyone seemed to shift at my words. They looked worried. I wasn't sure if they were worried about my ankle or worried if we would still be able to perform. Whatever the reason I knew I needed to fix it. There was no way I could let my team down so close to the end of the season.

"I'm fine," I said suddenly, as if saying the words would make it real. Before TJ could react to my words I attempted to stand up. It was a bad idea and left me screaming out in pain once again.

"Breathe, come on, deep breaths," TJ coached me, rubbing slow circles on my back to help me relax. "Once you calm down a little more we can see what's really going on."

"Here," a voice announced, then I felt cold ice pressed to my ankle. It was an instant relief.

"You're doing great," TJ told me as I managed to take normal breaths and stop crying for the most part. "Max, can you tell me where it hurts? I know it's your ankle, but is there a certain area hurting the most?"

"I don't know," I said honestly. Then, although I knew it was a bad idea I moved my ankle to feel where the stress and strain were most intense. I gave my answer through gritted teeth. "The outside of my ankle. And then kind of up my calf."

I instantly felt TJ move the ice to cover that area a little better. Even through the ankle brace and ace bandage, it was a comfort to feel the chill. A chill that seemed to go away the second TJ spoke. "We need to get you to the hospital. There's no way you can take the mat like this."

"What?" I exclaimed, possibly louder even then when I tried to stand on my already injured leg. "I have to perform."

"Max, I know you want to but you-"

"I have to," I tried again, cutting TJ off. "Just give me a minute and I'll be fine. I can wrap it up better and take some ibuprofen and then I can do it. Everyone's counting on me."

TJ stared at me for a long minute, taking in my face and the no doubt serious expression on it. He looked like he wasn't going to give in, but then I noticed he looked down and seemed to pause. It took me a second to realize he was likely looking at the necklace from my mom. When I told him about the necklace and the note, he told me how happy he was for me and also how proud my mom and everyone else would be to see me take the mat. And so, as I watched him looking at the small X and O that were hanging just below the neckline of my uniform, I knew he was going to let me give cheering a try.

"Let's see if you can even stand up," TJ finally said, clearly resigned to the idea of at least considering letting me take the mat.

With a nod, I reached forward to remove the ice from my ankle. Then, I grabbed onto TJ's hands that he was holding out for me to take. I stood up, putting all of my weight onto my left leg. Once I was standing upright, I slowly lowered my right leg to the ground, applying pressure to my ankle little by little. The pain was hard to ignore, but I knew it would take a lot more to stop me just yet.

"I need to get it wrapped better, but I'm okay," I assured him, still applying more and more pressure to my ankle gradually. Once I felt really brave, I stood on just my right leg, even flexing my foot to stand up on my tiptoes. "See, totally fine."

I knew TJ could see the pained look on my face while I was standing on my toes, but he didn't mention it. "Do you want me to call your dad to help?"

"No," I insisted with a shake of my head. "I don't want him to worry."

"Okay," he nodded then turned to the rest of the Nitro athletes standing nearby. "Can someone go with Max to the med station and get her ankle wrapped up?"

"Got it," Connor offered instantly, moving to stand next to me and wrap an arm around my waist. "Do you want me to carry you?"

"No, I can walk," I said to both him and TJ. "Thanks though."

"Alright," TJ began, still giving me an uncertain look. "Let's get back to warming up people. We only have a few more minutes until we take the stage."

CHAPTER 30

The last year I lived in Oregon I was playing soccer on a particularly rainy day and slipped while running. It was a normal enough occurrence, but as I was falling I twisted my body around wrong and landed on my wrist and arm. The sound of the bone breaking was loud, even louder than the other kids running around and yelling at my friend Ben to shoot the ball in the goal. Within seconds of landing in the mud, the game stopped and my dad raced towards me. I was in the hospital within what felt like minutes and in a cast not long after that. But I was determined to still play the rest of the season, and managed to do so without too much trouble. I just had to be careful not to hit my arm into anyone or anything for the first week or two. After that, I often forgot I was even injured.

My ankle injury going into our final performance wasn't quite the same. With the help of the medical team on site in the warm up room, I was able to get all taped and wrapped up so that my ankle would be able to make it through our time on stage. At least that was the hope. But, as I went back to warm-ups I could tell that not everyone was believing I would be able to handle the full routine. Many of the athletes on Nitro, as well as athletes from other gyms that were in the room when I tried my tumbling pass last, were looking my way as if I was going to fall to the ground again at any moment.

"Gather up everyone," TJ called out to the athletes in teal as we finally finished warming up. Or rather as everyone else finished warming up. I mostly stuck to simply stretching to get my ankle a bit more prepared for what was still to come.

"I know you all want to win today." TJ continued. "So do I. But today is not what defines us. This whole season has been a dream season for Nitro, and I couldn't be any prouder of each and every one of you. When you go out there I want you to show everyone watching what we're made of, but remember that win or lose we are a team. And win or lose I am blessed and honored to have each of you on this team. Now hands in one last time."

Around me, athletes in black and teal reached their hands in towards where TJ was standing at the center of the huddle. Then, just as we had so many times before, we called out the cheer that went before every performance. I said the words on autopilot, the sounds of the crowd suddenly reaching my ears. The team before us was beginning the dance portion of their routine, meaning we would be taking the stage any second. That meant that, ready or not, my ankle was about to be put to the test in a performance that mattered more than any other this season.

"Ready?" Emma asked me, holding a pinky out towards me.

"Ready," I nodded, taking her pinky with mine. I then placed my left hand on my new necklace for a second before reaching to take hold of Lilly who was walking my way. "Let's do this."

The next three minutes passed unlike any other time I had performed the routine. It was like my body was again running on autopilot again, this time taking the routine one move at a time. First, I focused on my standing jumps, followed by a basket. Then it was on to my first running tumbling and elite flying skills before more standing jumps. Every time I went to do a new portion of the routine I told myself it was just one more thing and then I would be that much closer to getting off my feet. But, it wasn't just about doing the motions, I still needed to perform and push myself to do the best I could for my team.

As I stood in the corner of the mat for the very tumbling pass that I fell while trying during warm-ups, I took a deep breath, then took off running three hard steps before beginning the punch front move. My body relied on muscle memory, flipping and spinning and twisting at just the right time. Then, as I neared the corner of the mat I pushed with my legs as hard as I could coming out of the whip before kicking my leg up as high as possible and began to twist my body. It wasn't until my feet landed on the mat that I realized I had completed the kick double. The landing was jarring, to say the least, but I knew I couldn't let it affect the squad.

Biting down on the inside of my cheek to keep from screaming out at the pain I was feeling, I did an overly sassy snap motion above my head to the audience before doing a hair flip and then turned to once again take off across the mat. This time I performed a much simpler pass, ending in a full then immediately going into a punch front at a slight angle so I was making my way towards the center of the mat where my stunt team was waiting. I followed the punch front with two back handsprings and a whip before finally ending the tumbling pass with a kick double. The pain as I landed was so intense I yelped before I could control it. Although it seemed that a few people on the mat noticed, the audience watching was unaware of what was really going on.

"Almost done Max," Matthew said to me as we prepared for the start of pyramid.

I had tears beginning to roll down my face and only hoped the audience and judges thought it was thanks to the perfect routine we were performing. Either way, I needed to focus on pyramid. Despite the new changes, I flew through the air easily, ignoring every twinge of pain I felt along the way.

When Matthew, Connor, and Juleah finally stood with me at the back of the mat, just seconds before the routine would be over, I focused on the fact that it was almost done. I ignored the searing pain as they picked me up and tossed me high into the air. Kicking my left leg as high as possible, I snapped it back before twisting my body in one full rotation. Then, I kicked my leg and began twisting yet again. Landing back in the arms of my friends who had just thrown me, I held my breath as if waiting for everything to fall apart.

"We did it!" I heard Emma yell, as she jumped and raced towards me while the audience clapped and cheered.

"What?" I asked, then screamed as my feet touched the ground. The pain in my ankle was making me see stars, and I was beginning to feel lightheaded.

"I got you Max," Connor assured me, instantly swooping me up into his arms.

As we began walking off stage I clutched onto him and cried, suddenly focusing on nothing but the pain I was feeling. Every step away from the mat caused a little more of my adrenaline to wear off, bringing me face to face with the damage that was clearly done. Something was majorly wrong with my ankle, but when I heard Matthew's words I knew it was worth it.

"We hit zero," he said, celebrating with the other Nitro athletes as we were finally off the mat and once again backstage. "We just won."

CHAPTER 31

Once we were off the stage, the tears and emotions didn't stop. Everyone around me continued to celebrate as the sound of the next team's music filled the arena, the excitement not wearing off easily. I, on the other hand, was struggling with the pain even without having any weight on my ankle. Despite my protesting at first, TJ found a wheelchair for me, as well as a massive bag of ice. First priority was getting me to my dad.

"I'm not leaving," I told him over and over as he talked to TJ about taking me to the hospital. "I don't care how bad it is, I need to stay. There's no way I'm missing awards."

"What if you broke it and it sets wrong?" he challenged me with the raise of an eyebrow.

"Then I'll try not to cry too loud when they set it again," I shrugged, although I knew it wouldn't be a pleasant feeling. "I have to be here Dad."

I could tell my dad didn't want to give in, but it was also clear he knew why I was so intent on staying. After all, awards were the real moment we had been waiting for. As team after team in our division took the stage we got more pumped about our performance. The other co-ed level 5 teams were performing great, but our level of difficulty was clearly higher than a few teams, and a few others had some stunting falls or tumbling errors that made it clear that winning was finally a reality. By the time the ten teams that made it to finals were sitting on the mat for awards, the nervous energy was palpable.

"This is it," I said to Connor and Emma who were sitting on either side of me.

Leaving my wheelchair at the edge of the stage for easy access when awards were done, I sat with Nitro in the left back corner, farthest from the edge of the stage. We were all holding hands, squeezing fingers, and fidgeting in our seats. Around us, other teams were doing the same. With every team announced, we were one step closer to the moment we had been waiting for all season.

"Alright everyone, time for the top three teams," the announcer spoke into his microphone. At his words, my hold on my friend's hands became a death grip. "First up, we have our bronze medal winners."

While the MC announced the team, causing a sea of grey and red uniforms to jump up and celebrate, I put my head down and tightened my grip on both Emma and Connor's fingers. One more team and we would be crowned. My ankle was the farthest thought from my mind in that moment.

"Up next, we have our second-place team, taking home the silver this year." He paused for dramatic effect. "From TNT Force, let's hear it for Nitro."

I looked towards the man who was speaking, certain I had heard him wrong. Around me, my teammates were doing the same. There was a mistake, he read the wrong team name, or it was some kind of joke. But, as I watched Matthew let go of Emma's hand and stand to take the trophy being held out to us, I knew it was real. Nitro lost. Despite everything I did, and all the hard work, we lost.

"I don't understand," I mumbled, my voice drowned out by the sound of the announcer calling out the name of the first-place team.

"But we should have won," Connor muttered, likely to himself.

Turning to look at Connor, I glanced past him and saw TJ standing in the corner of the stage, a look of complete disbelief and sorrow on his face. It was unlike anything I had ever seen, and before I thought better of it I stood up and began limping towards him for a hug. Despite feeling like I had cried out all my tears from my ankle pain during and after our performance, I instantly felt wet trails streaking down my face. Part of me knew it was a little childish, but as I heard TJ sniffle I took comfort in the fact that we all were feeling the same thing. And by all of us, I mean each member of Nitro that slowly made their way to TJ and joined in what quickly became a group hug.

I was reminded in that moment of another group hug we had shared. Months before, when Leanne was kicked out of the gym for bullying me, I was the center of a group hug after TJ broke the news to the rest of Nitro and their parents. This time, the situation was much different. No one was trying to comfort anyone, so much as simply find comfort by standing together in their misery. We were all at such a loss as to what to do or say, that only tears seemed to help.

"Let's get everyone together for a photo with your banner and trophy," an overly cheery voice called out. If it wasn't for her, we might have stood there crying all day. "Just a really quick photo and then we need to clear the mat."

Slowly, and with tears still falling, we stood together and took a few pictures, our smiles faked as best we could. There was a chance people who saw the photo would think we were crying happy tears at placing second, but everyone on the stage with us knew the truth. We were devastated. Plain and simple.

"Let's head off stage," TJ encouraged us, a frown still on his face. He looked like he wanted to say more, but instead just began walking off the blue mat.

The crying and hugging and general sadness continued off stage, none of us quite ready to find our parents and no doubt relive everything again. So instead we stood together and tried to make sense of everything that had just occurred. We came in second place, despite a perfectly executed routine. Instead of winning the title we were certain was ours, we were pushed aside while a different team celebrated with the trophy that should have been coming home with us.

"I don't understand," Emma said out loud, although not to any one person exactly. "How did this happen?"

"They always win," a voice said, catching my attention as well as those around me. We turned to see three athletes from our division. Their team came in fifth thanks to a few bobbled stunts during their pyramid. The girl that had spoken continued once she had our attention. "You guys won and everyone knows it. But the judges love the big gyms. They always do. So, you guys lose, and they win yet again."

"We know who really won today, though," one of the other athletes with her said, her face looking almost as sad as the members of Nitro. "You guys killed it, and it's not fair you didn't get first."

Just like that, the athletes turned and walked away. It was strange, but hearing them say what we were all thinking helped in some small way. We were still sad and generally upset, but we began making our way out to find our families and fellow TNT Force athletes. As we walked, or rather they walked and I rolled thanks to Connor pushing my wheelchair, I noticed others looking at us. Person after person glanced our way, giving us sad looks or turning to whisper something to people near them while pointing at us. Then, just before we turned the corner to where we were meeting everyone, a girl in a black and orange uniform stopped me.

"You're Max, right?" she asked, causing Connor to stop the wheelchair. When I nodded, she continued, "Did you really break your leg in warm-ups?"

"My ankle, but I don't know yet for sure," I shrugged. "I wanted to stay for awards."

"Well I hope you feel better soon," she said in reply. "Oh, and you totally should have won. Your tumbling alone was clearly the best."

I mumbled a thank you then glanced at Connor as he continued to follow the members of Nitro. He looked as confused as I felt, but neither of us knew what to say. Instead, we moved down the hallway until we were met with a wave of parents, friends, and family members waiting to greet us. Many of them were crying as they announced over and over again that we should have won. But, as my dad said those very words to me while dropping down beside me to give me yet another hug, I knew it didn't matter. Even if everyone sitting in the arena thought we should have won, we didn't. The trophy went to another team, and we were once again only good enough for second place.

CHAPTER 32

As I made my way to dinner later that evening with the assistance of crutches, I couldn't help but think back to just a year ago when I had attended the same dinner before beginning my week at Summit. I had gone to the pizza party, worried about what I would say to Connor, Matthew, Emma, Gwen, and my other friends that were on level 5 teams at TNT Force. None of them had ended up on top, and only Bomb Squad had placed in the top 3 of their division. So, as I finally reached the picnic tables covered in snacks, I felt a strange sense of déjà vu. Only this time, even with a few things to celebrate, the emotional pain was much worse than the year before when it was only my friends that were having a hard time processing everything that happened during finals.

"How's the ankle?" Gwen asked me as I plopped down onto the first seat I found open.

"It's still attached," I shrugged. My ankle was wrapped in a temporary cast that would stay on until I got an MRI once I was home. My dad didn't like that the hospital staff didn't let him help with their checking of my injury, so he was determined to wait for "better care" until he was "somewhere I trust" where he could "assist as needed." I may have rolled my eyes at him more than once while listening to his rant on the way home from the hospital.

"You've seen the posts on Instagram, right?" I nodded in reply to Gwen, instantly smiling despite all the not so great things I had gone through that day.

"I finally had to turn my phone off," I explained. "The posts are popping up nonstop, and I needed a break.

"You better get used to it," Connor suggested. He placed a full plate of pizza and chips in front of me before sitting down beside me with a plate of his own. "This is all just standard stuff for a cheerlebrity."

"Thanks," I said, although it was only for the pizza. "And I'm not a cheerlebrity. Just someone who refused to quit, even when I should have."

"Don't say that," Gwen corrected me. "The only thing people are talking about more than your injury is how Nitro should have won."

As Gwen got up to go refill her plate I couldn't help but admit she was right. The buzz on Instagram and Twitter since the small co-ed level 5 awards was all about Nitro. Partly about the fact that I had managed to perform the entire two-and-a-half-minute routine despite breaking my ankle in warm-ups. But mostly, thankfully, everyone focused on the fact that Nitro lost when anyone watching, including the athletes that came in first place, felt we should have won. At first, it was just random athletes posting how it wasn't fair that a well-known team beat a small gym. Then, little by little, other teams, coaches, and even a few judges began speaking up as well. And the posts only got more frequent when everyone learned that Nitro had only lost by less than a quarter of a point. It was causing a lot of people to claim the entire judging was rigged after the scores were tabulated, although it did little to ease the pain of losing.

"So, are you ready to head home?" Connor asked me, absentmindedly peeling pepperoni off his pizza and popping it into his mouth.

"I don't know," I said honestly. "I feel like we're leaving here with so much unfinished business. We didn't come here for second place."

"But it was a great second place," Matthew announced sitting down across from Connor and myself. "If you don't win, give them something to remember, right?"

"That sums it up pretty well," I laughed, unable to keep a straight face as Matthew shoved almost an entire slice of pizza in his mouth. "At least some of us get to leave champions."

My comment was made as more members of Detonators showed up and began taking even more photos with their first-place trophy. It should have made me feel bad to know they won while Nitro came in second and Bomb Squad finished in fourth, but it was also just nice to know TNT Force would finally be taking home a first-place Worlds title.

"Do you wish you were placed on Detonators now?" Matthew asked, following where I was looking.

"Maybe a little," I joked. "But only for a few seconds. Then I can't help but be happy how the whole year went. Like TJ said before we competed, one final performance and how the judges scored us doesn't define the whole season."

"I guess you're right," Matthew said with a sigh. "But it sure would have been fun to go out on top."

"Second place isn't exactly the bottom," Emma reminded him as she joined our table along with a few others.

While Emma and Matthew began going back and forth in their standard flirt-fighting about who was correct between the two of them, I looked around at the athletes and family members at the pizza party. There were no more tears, even if not everyone looked particularly happy. Which was a good first step. My dad, who was with other parents helping to pass out freshly made root beer floats, caught my eye with a little wave. He held up a full cup as if to ask if I wanted one, and in reply, I, of course, gave him a thumbs up. Knowing I couldn't exactly get up and go to him easily he walked over and placed the cup in front of me.

"You know what I think all you kids need?" my dad said, causing all the talking at our table to come to a stop. "A good pool party."

"Yes!" Matthew and Connor both agreed instantly.

Then, just like that, we began talking and planning it, as if the pool party was the most important thing in the world. Sure, I knew the emotions of getting second place and all that went with it were not forgotten for good. But, sitting with my friends and just having fun now that all the hard work was over felt pretty great. And, as I watched my dad walk back to his ice cream station, I knew I had people in my life that would be proud of me even if I had ended Worlds in last place. So, as I reached my hand up to play with the somehow familiar charms on my necklace, I smiled and assured myself yet again that second place wasn't really all that bad.

If you enjoyed this book, please take the time to write an honest review on Goodreads and/or Amazon. Your reviews and opinions are truly important to indie authors!

ABOUT THE AUTHOR

 Dana Burkey is a self-published author living in Bellingham, Washington. She has been enjoying her time in the Pacific North-West since 2009, making her move there after graduating from Youngstown State University in Ohio. She began self-publishing young adult fiction in August of 2014, and is most known for her TNT Force Cheer Series. Currently Burkey is enjoying performing improv, creating stories, and looking for life's next adventure.

A big thank you to Bows by April for the amazing bow on the cover. Order your own TNT bow, or many other at BowsByApril.com!

Order bows perfect for
Worlds, Summit, or all season
long from
CheerBowsBowtique

SNEAK PEEK

Continue reading for a sneak peek of book 4 in the TNT Force Cheer Series: Super Base. For more information about this book and others, or to rate the book you just read, be sure to check out Dana on Goodreads or Amazon.

CHAPTER 1

"Remember, you still need to take it easy," Connor reminded me as I stepped onto the blue air mat.

"Come on, you know me," I replied.

"Exactly," he laughed. "Take it easy."

Running three steps forward, I began a beyond basic series of moves for a level 5 cheerleader like myself. I performed a round off, my body flipping around thanks to a push from my hands, to land on both feet simultaneously for a nice transition into the next move. With extra height from the air mat boosting me into the air, I then did a back handspring. Usually I would follow it with a few more moves and end with a kick double full or another trick that was sure to get lots of points from judges. But, as Connor had said, I needed to take it easy. So, instead of going for something flashy I performed another backflip motion, this time tucking my knees into my chest as I went. The resulting move was a basic back tuck, which I landed before walking off the mat and back to where Connor was standing.

"See, I went super easy," I frowned, feeling rather lame for the skills I had just thrown.

"Super easy means you keep healing, remember?"

He emphasized his point by patting my head as he walked past me to step onto the mat I had just used. Then, as if to show off, he did his own running tumbling pass that was more at the difficulty I had wanted to perform. I didn't bother to watch him the whole time though, instead moving to go sit on one of the gym's blue performance mats to stretch. After all, stretching was one of the only things I could do without someone at the TNT Force Cheer gym reminding me to be careful and take it easy.

As much as the reminders from athletes and coaches bugged me, I knew they were right. After all, it hadn't even been four months since I broke my ankle bad enough to need surgery. I had a nice scar on the outside of my right ankle to remind myself of the whole ordeal, as well as the watching eyes of every athlete at the gym. Well, everyone at the gym as well as the world. The only difference was that when people around the world made comments, I could turn off social media notifications. When people at TNT Force said things, I had to nod and appear to be thankful for their advice.

"If you stretch too much more you might break in half," Connor told me, walking over to sit with me as I was holding a rather extreme body position. I was in a split to start, but then bent backwards over my right leg that was behind me. I was almost lying flat on my leg, my hands gripping my ankle to hold the move as long as possible.

"I doubt that," I assured him, pushing my body even flatter to deepen the stretch for emphasis.

Connor seemed to ignore me, instead focusing on drinking from his water bottle. Since he could actually go all out with his tumbling practice, there was a layer of sweat shining on his forehead which made his already black hair look somehow even darker. It didn't help that it was longer at the moment, the ends curling and sticking to his perspiration covered skin. Instead of a usual Nitro practice shirt he was wearing a thin grey tank top that was making his sweat stains grow and expand as he worked. It all made me feel even more annoyed I couldn't put in a real work out like he clearly had.

"Are you ready yet?" he asked me casually after I had been stretching a little longer.

"I guess so," I shrugged. "The usual?"

"Of course."

Hopping up off the floor, I stood in front of Connor, my back facing him. I was well over a foot shorter than him, so as he placed his hands on my waist he leaned closer to reach down far enough. His grip was firm without being too tight, instead making me feel reassured that he was going to do what he needed to in order to keep me from falling or getting hurt again. Locking my hands around his wrists, I counted us in before we began the warm up stunt we had been doing for weeks.

Bending my legs slightly, I pushed up with my feet as well as my hands as Connor tossed me straight into the air. Even if I hadn't pushed to help my ascent, I would have easily flown upward thanks to Connor's added height and muscles. I soared above the mat, keeping my body in a tight and straight line until I felt gravity kicking in and I began to fall. Only, I didn't have to fall far. Instead, Connor reached his arms up and grabbed onto my feet to keep me from moving any further. I squeezed my ankles together as tight as I could as I held my arms up in a simple high-v. Once a solid 10 seconds had passed, Connor counted down before giving me a slight push forward as he moved his hands away from my feet. He then took hold of my waist as I was falling, keeping me from landing too hard onto the blue mat.

"Single around?" I asked, placing my hands back on Connor's wrists.

"You don't want to try that again?"

"What do you think?"

I turned to look at Connor as I spoke, raising one eyebrow to show him my current mood at doing such basic stunts. In reply, Connor smiled down at me, his dimples making it almost impossible to stay annoyed at his suggestion for long. His expression made it clear he was only messing with me, so I turned away from him and prepared to be tossed up once again. This time I spun around in a full circle before he caught me above his head just as seamlessly as before. It was all so frustrating considering the stunts I knew I was capable of, but the steady increase was the only way I was allowed to take things, according to both my dad and my coach.

"I think you're about ready for something harder," Connor said to me an hour later. We had performed the same toss moves over and over again, and were finally sitting on the mat for a very necessary water break. "Maybe we can single leg on your left for a little bit at least. Then you can make sure you still have your balance."

"My balance is fine," I replied, my tone coming out a little harsher than I meant it to at first. "I just don't see why I can't go back to normal stunts and tumbling yet. Sure, I got hurt. But I'm fine. No pain, no swelling, and I'm keeping it wrapped. Nothing is going to go wrong."

"I feel like you said that at Worlds at some point," he teased.

I stuck my tongue out at him, then pulled out the cheer bow I could tell was sitting crooked on my head. It was a white bow with a Starbucks logo and 'I cheer a latte' written in green glitter. It matched my white tank top with the same logo and letters, as well as my green cheer shorts. I did the best I could to fix it without the use of the wall of mirror behind me. Once it was in place I laid back flat on the mat, more out of frustration than exhaustion.

"What's wrong?" Connor asked, likely in reply to the heavy sigh I let out once I was resting on my back.

"I just want things to be back to normal," I said, turning to look at him once he moved to lay down beside me.

"You don't have too much longer to wait," he reminded me. "In fact, I bet by camp TJ will let you do at least most of the skills."

"If not, I'll go crazy." I thought about it for a second before I continued. "Or more crazy. I already feel like I'm losing my mind every time I have to watch everyone do stunts and tumbling while I either do nothing or have to water it all down."

"A little waiting now will be worth it later," Connor said, his face more serious than it had been all through our practice time. His expression made his dark green eyes look more intense than usual. "You get hurt again and Nitro won't have any chance of making it to Worlds and showing everyone that we're so much more than a second place team. We should have won last year. So as much as it sucks right now, just think of how good Florida's going to be next year."

I nodded in reply, deep down knowing that what he was saying was true. Last season all felt like a build up to win Worlds, but in the end, we didn't make it happen. Coming in second place was great, but we had been certain the golden globe trophy and the rings were coming home with us. All of it made the athletes returning for the new season on the team that much more determined to get back out there and show the world what we could do. Which also meant I needed to stay healthy enough to be a part of everything. Even thinking about Worlds had made me eager to get back to work.

"Want to do a few more single arounds?" I asked.

"Sure," Connor agreed easily, obviously as determined as I was.

CHAPTER 2

"Do you think you'll get to fly for the showcase?" Lexi asked me later that evening as we sat around my pool enjoying the sunny Texas weather.

"I'm not sure," I said honestly. "TJ's been really strict with me. I'm not even allowed to throw basic tumbling during most practices, and any stunting I do is only at prep level or on two legs."

"It looks really good though," Halley offered, from the other side of me. "It's really easy to see you did a lot of core work over the summer."

"True, but I'm sure it still kind of sucks," Lexi noted. "I think I would go insane."

Halley nodded in agreement, and I found myself thankful that they both understood me so well. When I had told my neighbor Peter the latest update after getting home from the gym, he didn't seem to understand why I was so frustrated still. He was a great friend, but it really did take a fellow cheerleader to understand the struggles sometimes. Being on the mat wasn't enough when you knew you could do more, injury or no.

"So, I think I want to get my hair cut," Lexi said, changing the subject to one she had clearly been thinking about for a while.

"How short?" I asked, shocking myself. Just two years ago I could have cared less about things like hairstyles and makeup. But now, as a cheerleader, it was a part of my everyday life in so many ways. I was still a tomboy all the way, but I had little girly moments now and then thanks to my time spent around rhinestones, mascara, and the like.

"As short as yours," Lexi replied, giving me a worried expression.

"You should, it's so much less work to deal with," I encouraged her. Her expression instantly turned to a grin, clearly relieved I was okay with her copying my haircut.

"What if I said I was thinking about cutting my hair too?" Halley chimed in quickly. "I've been thinking it will help me look more mature now that I'm on a senior team."

"Then we would all match!" Lexi all but shouted, clearly loving the idea.

And I had to admit, I liked the idea as well. I got to know Lexi and Halley before I even joined the gym, meeting them at the local indoor trampoline park. I had been impressed with the tricks they were performing, otherwise I never would have talked to people so different from myself. The first time I met them they had been covered in head to toe rhinestones and glitter while I was wearing basketball shorts and an old faded shirt. But before long I was cheering with them at TNT Force, and had somehow bonded with them despite being so different.

We didn't just dress differently either. I stood out like a sore thumb around my friends. They were both super hard to miss with their bright blond hair, thankfully natural unlike some cheerleaders I had met during my time at gym. Not only that, but they also managed to look fancy all the time thanks to their expertly applied makeup. Even while we were tanning and swimming for the day, Lexi had on eyeliner to help her bright blue eyes pop, and Halley made sure to wear a white tankini so it brought out her tan skin and brown eyes even more. I, on the other hand, was like a less polished version of them.

Sure, I had on a pink and green swimsuit that was similar to the one Lexi was wearing, but I wasn't what most people would consider cute. I was short and tiny despite my muscles from cheer, but my short cropped brown hair, thick eyebrows, and blue-green eyes made me look more tough than sweet any day.

"Having matching hair would make for some great pictures this season," I added, focusing on the planning once again. "It will help us look better in photos even though we'll all have on different uniforms."

"For now," Lexi said, a gleam in her eyes.

"You're really going to talk to TJ?" I asked her, knowing instantly what she was referring to.

"I have to," she all but whined. "I mean, I love that we have a junior restricted 5 team now, but I want to be on Nitro with you so bad. And if Catherine's struggling on flying then I can totally replace her."

"But then you two will be on a team without me," Halley chimed in. "I mean, purple and teal look great together for photos, but I'll serious be jealous when you two both get to go to Worlds."

"That's if we both get to go," Lexi quickly reminded her. "I still have to actually make it on the team."

"Besides, you were both on the same team without me last year," I reminded Halley.

"Oh yeah," she said with a thoughtful look. "But being on a different team than us let you go to Worlds. So, it's not exactly the same thing as both of you going without me."

Halley continued trying to make her point for a few more minutes, then gave up to simply enjoy the sun. After all it was way too hot to do much more than lay around and relax. Despite it being the middle of August, it was just as hot as it had been all summer. Which was the only good thing about being restricted at cheer from my injury. Much like last summer every Nitro practice began with a THREE mile run before conditioning and then a grueling team practice. I still joined the team for most of the conditioning, but my coach wasn't letting me run just yet.

"You can walk one lap if you want," TJ had explained to me once I was cleared for light duty by my doctor. "But if I see you run even a step I'll make you a bonafide water girl for the next three months."

My coach was tough, but also had my best interests in mind. Or at least that's what my dad told me when I complained that evening. The truth was, I felt like running was going to help my ankle. Sure, it might push it a little too hard too soon, but after sitting out and watching assessments and then team placements from the sidelines, I felt like I was somehow cheating. Being placed on a top team at the gym without proving myself since the final performance at Worlds felt unfair to me. The only thing I could do about it, however, was heal faster so I could get on the mat and show everyone what I was still capable of.

"When do you go to the doctor again Max?" Lexi asked, as if reading my mind.

"Thursday. It can't get here fast enough."

"Do you think you'll be cleared after that?" Halley asked, sitting up on her deck chair to look at me while I replied.

"I don't know," I said with a sigh. "It's only a matter of time before TJ lets me start trying more stunts and tumbling at practice, but it's weird. There's a little part of me that's worried when I go to do the skills, I'll mess up."

"After an injury like you had I wouldn't be surprised if you have some trouble," Halley nodded. "Not that I want you to deal with that or anything. I've just seen it happen a lot."

"Exactly. Like when Cassidy came back to the gym."

Lexi's comment made me instantly more worried, my mind jumping to not only images of my surgery scar, but also the one I had seen after my gymmates' injury my first season cheering. Cassidy had been a flier on Fuze, TNT's senior level 4 team. But, when she fell and broke her collarbone I filled in for her to end the season. Everyone assumed she would come back and be back on Fuze or even a Worlds team before too long, but when she showed up for assessments just over a year later she struggled to even do basic tumbling and was too afraid of falling to try getting lifted again. Instead she was placed on a much lower level team based on her now more limited skills. I felt a cold chill race up my spine, instantly nervous I might share her fate.

"You don't need to worry though Max," Lexi assured me. "You're still tumbling fine, and from all the Snapchats you post while you and Connor practice it looks like you're getting a lot done."

"A lot of what exactly we aren't sure," Halley said quickly before both her and Lexi began giggling.

"My flying's not that bad," I reminded them.

"That wasn't what I meant," Halley began, only to get cut off by Lexi.

"Do you have ice cream? I think I might die if I don't eat ice cream right about now."

"This is my house we're talking about here," I began slowly for dramatic effect. "Of course we have ice cream. Now do you want chocolate fudge with that or butterscotch sauce."

"Is both an option?" Lexi grinned.
"Always."

CHAPTER 3

      Walking into the gym the following morning I noticed Lexi was not only already at the gym, but already in the office talking to TJ. I walked through the room, all the way down to the mat Nitro would be performing on for the day. The TNT Force gym was made up of four blue mats, all spring-loaded for all star cheerleading. They came complete with a wall of mirrors for athletes to see how they looked during practice along with a set of cubbies just off the floor for storing backpacks and water bottles. On the other side of the long rectangular room was first and foremost an office. It was made up of a few smaller rooms where each of the three owners TJ, Nicole, and Tonya could do paper work when they weren't out coaching.

Attached to that was an aptly named 'viewing room' which was the only place parents could stay to watch practices. The large picture window also kept all comments from affecting practices in any major way. Beyond that were the bathrooms, the much-used water fountain, and then an area filled with trampoline tracks, air mats, and even a foam pit where athletes could work on their running tumbling skills.

The room looked exactly how it had when I first entered the gym just two years prior, only now I was much more at home. I no longer tugged at the hem of my tight cheer shorts or felt self-conscious with a glittery bow in my hair. Instead, I fit in with the team around me, all of us clad in teal and black practice uniforms expertly adorned with rhinestones to spell NITRO across the front of our sports bras or tank tops. The only thing that made me stand out at all was the black brace I slipped on my foot before trading my usual tennis shoes for a pair of white cheer shoes. It wasn't as hefty or as serious as the cast, boot, or brace that came before it, but it was still a little reminder to me and everyone around me that I was on limited cheer duty.

"Can I borrow a hair tie?" Emma asked, rushing up to me as I slid my tennis shoes into the cubby with my other stuff. Her hair was flopping around her head in a strange formation, likely hinting a broken rubber band.

"I think so," I nodded, digging through the bottles of Tylenol, extra cheer clothes, and granola bars in my bag.

"Thank you," she announced, pulling the hair tie from my hand before I could even extend it to her. Instead she took it and raced off to the mirror where she got to work pulling her long curly blonde hair up into a high ponytail before putting her bow back in place. Although the bow had an elastic band to keep it secured, it was never good enough to hold everything where it needed to stay during a long practice. Even for someone like me with short hair pulled into a half ponytail, using an extra elastic to keep the hair out of my face was a must at cheer.

"You're a lifesaver," Emma said as she returned to give me a thank you hug. "How's the ankle today?"

"Great," I said honestly. "Not that it means I'll be doing much."

"For now," she reminded me, giving her hazel eyes a roll for emphasis. "You'll be back in no time, making all of us remember why you're point flier."

Although the comment could have been taken as mean coming from some people, I knew Emma meant it in the best way possible. Emma was one of my best friends on Nitro, and as a fellow flier we got along great since we dealt with a lot of the same struggles. When I needed help getting the correct body position for a new skill,

Emma was always quick to help me figure it out. And when she needed ways to get extra height on a tumbling skill, I was always sure to let her know what worked best for me. It helped that she was dating Matthew, who was not only my stunting partner last season, but also Lexi's older brother. Those two factors meant her and I spent a lot of time together both inside and outside of the gym.

"How did stunting yesterday go with Connor?" Emma asked, giving her eyebrows a little wiggle.

"Fine," I shrugged. "It was just such basic stuff I was ready to pull my hair out. I mean, if I don't at least try to throw harder skills, we'll never know if my ankle is getting stronger or not."

"Soon," she assured me. "As annoyed as you are with having to mark skills and walk out tumbling passes, TJ is even more so. It's not exactly easy to see how everything is going to look without everyone actually in the air. He'll be just as glad as you when you're back at one hundred percent."

"I don't know about that," I frowned.

"Don't know about what?" Juleah asked, walking up to us while twisting her long black micro braids into a bun.

"Max's just stressing about getting back to normal," Emma said summing it up concisely.

"You and me both."

As my back base for stunts for the second year in a row, when I didn't go up into the air it meant Juleah didn't get to practice full out either. Instead she had to go through the motions, then work with other fliers in her extra time at the gym so she didn't get rusty. But, despite all that, she always had a smile on her face and a positive attitude before every practice. Like most of the athletes on Nitro, it was the persevering through rough times that made us really get the fuel to perform.

Our conversation continued a little as we began our pre-practice stretching, Emma and I holding positions a lot more extreme than Juleah. We were joined by more and more athletes in black and teal over time. And eventually the other 19 members of the team took seats around us. The team was still two people short, due to the open spots caused by injury and other commitments. Aaron hurt his knee a few weeks into summer conditioning, and Paula decided to take the season off to focus on high school cheer. Even though Paula wasn't a flier I found myself hoping Lexi could take the flying position so Catherine could fill in as a base for Paula instead. When TJ walked up to the practice mat without her though, I had a feeling their discussion didn't go how my friend was hoping it would.

"Okay everyone, time to get running," TJ called out. "I need to see Max and Sara K. The rest of you can get started."

"What's up Coach?" Sara asked as we both walked up to TJ.

"Max, how do you feel about giving running a try today?" He asked in reply to the question.

"I feel great," I replied enthusiastically. "I'm ready to go."

"Good, but you're running with Sara and a mile and a half only though." TJ paused, as if to let everything he had just said sink in. "You go at her speed, and don't push the pace like I know you will. If you feel any pain you quit and walk back. But if you make it through and it's all okay, then today we get to add in baskets."

I stared at TJ, my mouth all but hanging open. The offer to do baskets was enticing to say the least, and even the idea of getting to run was great. It showed he was going to let me start easing back into the full extent of the routine. But, running with Sara K was going to require all of my self-control. Sara was a great base, good at tumbling, and honestly a great addition to Nitro after moving up from Fuze after assessments. The problem was, running wasn't her thing. From day one she had always been the last person to finish the daily three miles. Her time wasn't terrible, it was just much slower than I could and would go when given the chance.

"It won't be that bad Max," Sara said, almost sounding a little hurt. "It's only two laps, so maybe I can go a little faster."

"That's not what this is about," TJ interjected. "I'm not trying to get you to go faster Sara. You try your best. Plus, your lap time is getting shorter every week. The reason I'm putting you girls together is so Max doesn't push herself like I know she will when left to her own devices. Look at it this way, after today you can tell everyone you did the conditioning run as fast as Max."

"Now that's kind of fun," Sara agreed, a hint of a smile growing on her face. "Think you can keep up Max?"

"Let's hope so," I said with a shake of my head, trying to have a good attitude about everything. Mostly because I knew that after the rather slow laps I would get to finally do some real flying. Which was a step in the right direction.

CPSIA information can be obtained
at www.ICGtesting.com
Printed in the USA
LVHW041127130523
746915LV00019B/147